MIND
YOUR OWN
MURDER

PERSEPHONE PRINGLE COZY MYSTERIES: ONE

PATTI LARSEN

To the amazing woman, writer, editor and friend who says yes over and over again.

Thanks, Kirstin!

ISBN: 978-1-989925-76-8

CHAPTER ONE

I was pulling off the interstate when my phone rang and, despite the fact it didn't interfere with my GPS's faithful guidance, I scowled and caught myself squinting at the interruption, nonetheless. Because, frankly, I was turning into my mother despite the fact there was no way I was now fifty. Dear God in Heaven, *fifty*.

Who needed the reminder? Besides, age was just a number. Right? If I told myself that over and over again, would it ever be true?

Delusions of youth began long before the big 5-0 rolled around, so I figured I was a lost cause in the growing-up department regardless.

"Yes, darling," I answered the caller, refusing to be one of those people who turned their radio down when they were trying to focus because *fifty*. I much preferred twenty-five. Thirty, max. "Did you need something or are you just checking up on me?"

My daughter's snort laugh made me grin despite myself. "You did abandon me for some mid-life crisis, post-divorce adventure, Mom. The least you could do is pretend to be brokenhearted I'm not with you."

My turn to laugh. "You'd hate it," I said, the stop sign at the end of the rather bland grassy exit merely a suggestion as I rolled through and turned right when the deep and sexy voice of the GPS my darling girl programmed for me before I left for said adventure suggested I do so with such seduction I heard her giggle. "Much like I'm beginning to despise good old Ryan or Chuck or whoever this guy is you've infected my GPS with."

Calliope gasped on the other end of the line. "*Mom*," she said, while I pictured her adorable cheeks rounding when she grinned, my daughter far more her father than me, at least physically. "He's *dreamy*."

"*Callie*," I used her exact chiding tone, "he's not *real*." I smirked to myself with a bit of wickedness, catching the crow's feet around my eyes in the rearview and refusing to give them another second of notice. I earned them, every one. "Unless you can hand me a live guy who sounds like that, keep your hands off my tech."

"Mom!" How had I raised a prude? My daughter's laughter had that refreshing breeze effect it always did, though her father's influence meant she acted far closer to my age than I did. "You were just divorced like a hot minute ago. Shouldn't you maybe wait for a bit before thinking about other men?"

She had so much to learn and hopefully never would because I wished her a far more fulfilling married life than I had. "Wait for what approximate amount of time that you may deem appropriate, my sweet? A month? Six? The rest of my life." She didn't respond, so likely she'd have rathered I stayed celibate and her version of the mother she remembered forever and ever. I wasn't so out of touch I wasn't aware it had to be hard for her, thinking of her mother in these terms. I still struggled a little knowing my own mother dated after Dad died, despite the fact she'd been remarried to Ralph for the past three years. Calliope would, however, have to get used to the fact her newly single mother wasn't about to waste another second. "You know we separated for a year before that, darling," I sing-songed the truth with far more relief and joy than I planned, "and I was single for a decade, whether you like it or not. I have no interest in shacking up with another roommate, so get over it." I relented a little because she was ever so quiet, and I might have pushed her too far. "But yes, if you say so." Sigh. More nothing. She'd learned the silent treatment from none other than the other half of her parent duo. "Speaking of which, how's your father?"

"So, you *do* care." Got her talking again, fabulous. The light tone of her voice reminded me she was more than likely distracted and any guilt I felt over the situation probably settled in the only me range these days. Calliope might have been mostly her father, but she was me, too, and rarely held grudges. Hard to balance my feelings with second-guessing hers all the time, though, when I knew better. Teasing or not, however, part of me wondered if Calliope held out hope Trent and I would somehow miraculously find our way back to each other when the exact opposite was true. At least, on my part.

Trees thinned on the left, the ocean glinting occasionally through the spruce trees lining the road. I noted the town sign welcoming me to Zephyr, Maine, which, according to said garishly painted signage, claimed to host the biggest flower festival in the state. While only a few hours' drive from my home in Wallace, it felt like a whole world away and exactly what I'd been hoping for.

"He's fine, Mom," she said, answering the question I'd already forgotten I'd asked. "Lonely, I think." She had to sound sad about it, tickling my guilt again. It's not like I abandoned him or her. They were both grown adults with their own lives and ambitions. Couldn't I have mine, too? "He misses you. We both do. It's not the same without you around."

She wasn't just talking about right now, either. I'd moved into the in-law suite meant for Mom down the road the same day I told Trent I wanted a divorce. And then to my new place three months ago. I might have been only a couple of miles from them physically, but Calliope felt the distance and had no qualms bringing it up.

More guilt. Thanks, kid.

"We agreed you'd stay with your father while you finish your summer semester and I'd run away for a month to celebrate my freedom, and everyone would be happy." I slowed to the requisite forty miles per hour. Which meant I set the cruise to fifty, naturally.

Calliope sighed heavily into the phone, that teenaged angst carried over to her early twentysomething existence like an old sweater

I hoped she'd grow out of before she turned into Trent for real. "You mean *you'd* be happy," she said, uncharacteristic resentment waving a red flag that had me frowning. "Sorry, Mom," she said then. "It's not your fault, I know that. I'm just worried about you." Yup, Trent through and through. "And about Dad. You know he needs someone to take care of him."

She wasn't kidding. Did he *ever*. While my ex might have been Very Special Agent In Charge Trent Garret to the real world, superhero crimefighter who led his own team and *everything* (insert sarcasm here), the man could barely find his socks in the morning, let alone let go of his need to control everything around him while missing the point over and over again. Not bitter or anything, just over and done with being last on his list while I put my family first. "Did you sign him up for that dating app you were talking about? The one for old people?" I didn't snort, I swear. Okay, maybe a little.

"He didn't want me to," she said. "I think he's still holding out hope, Mom."

"My darling girl," I said, all amusement gone, the sight of the edge of town now in view and my speed slowing at last to the limit thanks to traffic ahead, "I've been nothing but clear with you and your father since day one. I've

moved on, baby. It's time your dad did, too."
The idea of being with Trent again in any
romantic capacity? Made me anxious and
honestly revolted, though I'd never tell him
that. Not that over ten years of celibacy in our
marriage hadn't been an excellent indicator, as
far as I was concerned.

Old frustration sizzling, I turned off the air
conditioning and powered down my windows,
letting the sea breeze wash away the tension
and the past. "Callie, there will come a time you
fall in love. And then out of love. I hope you
realize it and accept it and let go long before
your father and I did." Twenty-four years of
my life with someone who was such a good
person, just not my person, still knotted my
insides with regret I knew better than to hang
onto. So why was I? It was called being human,
though I was working on that, too. "Trust me,
when he finds a girlfriend, he'll be so much
happier, and we can both move on." Meaning
my only child, of course, could let go of this
fantasy and drop the guilt trips already.

Because for me, moving on happened a
long time ago.

It was my turn at the stop sign, the adorable
main street of town finally getting my attention,
multi-colored storefronts and light traffic,
most of it pedestrian, drawing the most

satisfied smile from me. Someone had painted a chain of daisies on the pavement, marking the edge of the crosswalk with a fresh vine of adorable flowers that instantly lifted my spirits. This was going to be the perfect retreat and exactly what I needed. I was still positive of that fact as I pulled ahead to clear the intersection.

Forced to slam on the brakes when a sedan ignored the four-way stop and almost ran right into me.

Heart pounding, the gasp I uttered followed by Calliope asking if I was okay while, to my utter shock, the tall, thin man in the offending vehicle got out, red-faced and visibly livid, approaching my SUV with enough fury in his entire being. I was floored to realize he blamed me for the near accident.

Something he proceeded to scream at me in near incoherence while my startled brain fought to process the fact. It wasn't until he drew close enough to be an actual physical threat, I realized my windows were down. And, as was often the case, my snarky side won over self-protection in the face of his bullying behavior.

When he drew a breath to continue, in the silence of that moment, I acted (reacted), whipping out a business card and offering it to him through the open window.

"Persephone Pringle," I said, "holistic therapist. Looks like you have some anger management issues tied to a narcissistic overreactionism typically based in childhood trauma."

Oh, yes, I *did*.

He gaped at me a moment in shock, and actually took the card, too.

"I'm on a retreat," I went on, "but if you want a session, I'll make time since cases like yours usually mean isolationism and conflict with those around you." I really should have stopped talking, I know. But I found confronting those in high-octane meltdowns with calm and confidence often diffused them long enough to shut off their reaction. Case in point. Though, it was clearly not over for him, even if it was for me.

"Tourists," he snapped, physically shaking in anger. "Go home and leave us alone!" With his last word delivered, he retreated to his own car, astonished drivers in other vehicles watching with raised eyebrows when he flashed me a very rude gesture with his middle finger before peeling off again.

"Mom." Calliope's breathlessness mirrored my own. "Are you okay? What happened?"

Typically, anger filled in the seams when I

was confronted with conflict, something I'd never been proud of and continually worked on but had yet to master. Which was why I found myself gritting my teeth and clutching the steering wheel in frustration while I forced calm into my voice.

"Just a local yahoo with an attitude," I said. "It's fine." It was. *It was.* "Listen, honey, I'm going to find my place and get settled." I was not going to let that crazy guy's attitude ruin the first day of the rest of my glorious life. "I'll call you tomorrow."

"Love you, Mom," she said.

"Love you, too." I hung up, forced myself to relax, release the tension in my shoulders, the adrenaline burning off in my system. This was the new beginning I had dreamed of, four luxurious weeks all alone, to work on me, and only me, in the most deliciously selfish and self-affirming way possible.

Mr. Meltdown could suck it.

Be the bigger person, Persephone Pringle.

CHAPTER TWO

The sultry British boy Calliope saddled me with offered a breathless, "You've arrived at your destination," as I pulled into the short drive of the adorable little beach house I'd rented for the month, a soft ding finally ending the torture that was my daughter's tampering. I scowled at my phone, index finger tapping the screen a little harder than was necessary, shutting off the GPS app with satisfaction akin to self-righteousness. Promising myself I'd change the guiding voice to a more sedate and confident female before heading home, I keyed the window closed before shutting down the SUV and sitting for a moment, admiring the view.

Every home on the short side road that led me to the water had been painted an Easter egg color, from pink to pale blue, icy green and lavender, almost non-existent front lawns tiny patches of immaculate clover mixed with purple thyme, the front of the cottage lined in white-painted flower boxes bursting with hanging blossoms of a variety of colors and kinds, entire face a sunporch of windows reflecting the afternoon sunlight. I stepped out into the warmth of the late June day, inhaling the mixed scent of flowers and sea air, all my troubles vanished in that single breath.

Yes. Exactly as promised. This was going to be perfection.

My suitcase rolled noisily along the fresh asphalt, my purse and carry bag over one shoulder as I headed for the side entry at a lean, knowing I'd brought too much with me, that my shopping habit meant I'd be using less of what I packed and more of what I found to purchase, but unable to restrict my choices when I traveled. Something Trent always hated, and I now indulged perhaps a bit too much and on purpose.

A girl could never pack too many shoes, right? Or snub her nose too many times at the way things used to be.

I ignored the white-painted gate at the side of the house for now, leading to the side of the cottage and likely the garden beyond. I'd perused the photo spread on the site where I'd found the place enough times, I was sure I could find my way around without any assistance, small enough for easy care and yet picturesquely intimate.

Just what the doctor ordered. Or the therapist. I wasn't always one to follow my own advice, but this time I was all in.

A cute little wooden plaque trimmed in brass hung next to the door, greeting me with my retreat's name, Sunshine Cottage, 14 Daisy Lane. Ideal, really, the pale yellow paint and white trim making that name a lovely fit. I glanced toward the gate, the hedge and fence enclosing the entire backyard, excited by the privacy, and access to the beach I could just see over the rear of the property. While I'd studied the supplied images so I'd have the lay of the land, I had to admit the photos didn't do it justice, as was often the case. With the afternoon sun shining down, the soft sound of the ocean over the fence and the lure of the cottage interior, I found myself sighing in contentment. Funny, I'd never been here before, but I could feel myself settling in even prior to setting foot across the threshold.

The moment I reached for the doorknob, it opened without my help, the tall, smiling man on the other side beaming at me as I blinked in startled surprise.

"Persephone?" He reached out and shook my hand in aggressive friendliness, relieving me of my carry bags though I didn't ask for assistance, backing up and allowing me to trundle my suitcase over the doorway and into the sunroom. "Mitch Arbor, so happy to have you. Welcome to Zephyr and Sunshine Cottage!"

His enthusiasm, while appreciated, was going to be too much in very short order. Considering his presence had shattered my idyllic daydream of just me and the cottage and peace, I had to remind myself not to resent the poor man for just doing his job. I did smile in return, though, even as I hoped he'd meander off in the next few minutes and leave me to my dreamy retreat.

"Nice to meet you in person, Mitch." I let him take hold of my suitcase handle, shrugging to myself despite the tug on my internal control freak who was perfectly capable of wrangling her own bags and didn't need a man to do anything for me, thank you very much.

I'd be dealing with that demon attitude over the next few weeks.

"You're my first rental this month," Mitch said, passing through the narrow sunporch with its white wicker furniture and windows that I'd be opening to the lane for quiet evenings of sunset watching. The interior of the house felt a little dim after the bright white of the front room, but I quickly adjusted, admiring the plain but comfortable cottage décor, shiplap on every wall, short ceilings making the place feel cozy. "So, I double-checked everything when I opened the cottage yesterday, but if there's anything that needs refreshing, please just let me know."

I passed him, the hardwood floors catching the sunlight as I stepped into the brighter kitchen, pink fridge a retro chubby appliance I fell instantly in love with, small island perfect for cooking, the back door luring me out to the garden and the beach beyond.

"This is just lovely, Mitch," I said, turning back to him and smiling for real. "Thank you so much. I'm excited about my stay."

Mitch's prominent Adam's apple bobbed enthusiastically, tall, thin body hunched just a little though there was no threat of touching the ceiling despite his height and their lack thereof. He set my bags down on the floor, righting the suitcase with his other hand, before retrieving keys from his pocket and handing them to me.

"I'm happy to show you around," he said, nice tenor leaving the offer open.

"I'm fine," I said, already moving, one hand gentle on his arm, guiding him to the door. "I'd love to explore on my own if that's all right?" He bobbed a nod, though looked a little disappointed. "I'll let you know if I need anything, but it's been a long drive and I'd like to get settled in."

"Of course." Mitch paused with one foot over the threshold, then shrugged a little. "Have a great stay, Persephone."

I waved as he left, trying not to feel guilty. The poor man. Perhaps he was lonely and looked forward to greeting new guests? Not my problem, I had to remind myself. And, if necessary, I'd make it up to him, invite him for lunch one day just to be friendly.

Eep. Wait a second. Not too friendly, though, right? I know what Calliope would have suggested, teased me about. Gave myself a headshake and a deep breath. Not every man I met was a potential partner, for goodness sakes. Hopefully, he hadn't gotten the wrong impression. Surely, I'd been nice but dismissive? Would inviting him to dinner to thank him for the space imply the wrong thing?

Yikes. I hadn't thought about it this way before, caught myself a bit flat-footed by the notion. Didn't make me want to change my mind or go back to the way things had been or anything like that. On the contrary. Calliope's teasing about dating obviously woke something in my mind if I was spinning out of control like this over absolutely nothing. Was I ready to date after all? Did I even want to find someone? Unlike Trent, I was perfectly capable and more than happy on my own. Wasn't I?

Well now, more issues to deal with on this retreat, apparently. Being single was going to take some real navigation.

The only bedroom's canopied queen-sized bed had me swooning over the netting that added such a romantic air, the clawfoot bathtub under a large window a dreamy promise of long soaks under moonlight. I discarded my bags in the bedroom for now, purse joining me in the kitchen, its casual home now the back of a stool while I finally opened the rear door and stepped out into the garden.

While the fence blocked a lot of the view, I appreciated the privacy it offered. The small deck had plenty of space for me, a bistro set with cast iron chairs and a round table suggesting coffee and sunrises as much as the front porch beckoned me to enjoy sunsets. A water feature burbled in the far corner, fountain in the shape of a trio of lily pads cascading a trickle down into a little pond surrounded by flowers and an irregular stone walkway.

Perfect, all of it. Every single last piece of the puzzle slid into place, serenity and solitude and the chance to figure out where to go from here without interruption or my family and their needs wrapping me in guilt and distraction.

I was still Calliope's mom. Trent's friend and ex. I didn't want the connection I had to them to end. I just needed it to change. And while it was impossible to have them do the changing unless they chose it, I could. Wanted to. Planned to go home a brand new me.

Just a few minor details (snort) to deal with first.

I did mention I was a control freak. And the fact the single lawn lounger sat under the shade of the tall oak tree wouldn't do. I'd be dragging it out the back gate to the beach in short order. And the rather creepy trio of garden gnomes staring up at me from the bottom step would be finding new homes for the duration of my stay.

Otherwise? This was exactly what I'd hoped for, and I couldn't wait to forget everything and just enjoy the peace, quiet and solitude for the next four glorious weeks.

"I hate you!"

Please. Tell me I didn't speak too soon.

CHAPTER THREE

I was tempted to retreat back inside, to avoid and ignore the argument now unfolding in the backyard just over my garden fence to the left. The last thing I wanted was to be sucked into other people's problems at this juncture. Considering this month was meant to be my own personal retreat into what ailed me, helping others with their issues, while something I loved and a career that fulfilled me, wasn't part of the present plan.

It was obvious to me, however, as the young woman's voice crackled with hurt, answered by muffled shouting from a male individual, their decision to yell out their pain wasn't going to go away anytime soon and nor did it sound like something new. In fact, as the man's voice grew more distinct, it was apparent to me from the rather repetitive insults and unimaginative narrative they shared, (along the lines of, "Don't you talk to me that way, young lady!" and "You never listen to anything I say!") this was likely an ongoing issue.

One I really didn't want to have to live with for the next four weeks. Which had me peeking over the fence to at least identify my neighbors if not interact with them all to better avoid them in the future if need be.

The *oh crap* moment I endured as the tall, angry man emerged from the back door of the neighboring house to confront the young woman in their own garden had me suddenly doubting my luck and choice of residence after all. Surely the Universe wasn't so unfair as to dump such troubles in my lap when all I wanted was a little peace and solitude? But no, apparently the joke was on me, because, when my cranky neighbor stopped on the top step of their cottage, his red face no less furious than when he'd almost hit me at the stop sign, I identified with an inward sigh of disgust the tourist hating terrible driver who'd made me feel most unwelcome.

Continued to, despite myself. Clearly, his temperament hadn't improved and, if the confrontation of screaming, shouting, near incoherent back and forth I now witnessed was any indication, that state of mind had to be his default. A default that continued to spill over into my garden despite the fence because no amount of white picket, tightly planked or not, could keep that level of obnoxious behavior from soaring over the top to include everyone in earshot.

Everyone in the *state*. I bet Calliope would be calling me in short order to ask me what they were yelling about.

While I'd encountered the man prior to this, his conflict companion was a total stranger. She had similar features, however, her own face lit with that bright pink topped by a faint sheen of moisture that arose in moments of loss to rage I could only imagine had been brought on by proximity to the arrogant aggression of the man who loomed over her.

Her father, had to be. Only dads talked to grown daughters that way.

"As long as you live in this house," he boomed then, confirming it all over again, shaking a finger at her, so very paternal and on the level of bad parenting I usually had to unravel with years of therapy, "you'll do as I say, young lady!"

Classic Dad move, with a proven track record to send even the most docile and kindly of young people into a frenzy of rebellion. I'd seen it a million times before, had to moderate it on spare occasions between Calliope and Trent despite the fact our kid was as close to good and kind and well-behaved as anyone I'd ever met and probably didn't deserve. Still, conflicts happened. This case, however, had me guessing that their entire relationship had been built on a crusty, crumbling foundation of hurt and pushback that would likely mean a lonely estrangement for both of them in the not-too-distant future. All the signs were there, the walled-off body language, the jutting aggression, the invisible wall of hurt between them. He bore an air of someone on the brink of breaking his connection to his kid once and for all, like most her age, wanting freedom and approval in equal measure, made worse and deeply wounding when neither were forthcoming. His daughter was no different, her slim body rigid with denial as she tossed her hands in the air, palms slapping the thighs of her white shorts loudly enough to make me jump when they fell.

"I'm a grown adult, Dad," she snapped. "You can't tell me what to do."

Oh boy, saw that coming, almost whispered it out loud because it was the final blow in many an arsenal, but never with the kind of result desired because last stands built out of old anger usually blew back into the face of the angry. That kind of response never ended well for either party, the receiver damaged as much as the attacker. I struggled to step off, to disengage from the scenario, my natural affinity to want to help at war with the selfish nature of my choice of personal venues for the month. It was pretty apparent, however, that choice dropped me into the sort of turmoil I happened to be uniquely educated and inclined to deal with, worse cases than this one ending in positive outcomes giving me hope and faith in my methods if not their willingness to fully reconcile.

I'd had one hope in all this, a hope he dashed with his "under my roof" line. Any chance perhaps he was just visiting and didn't actually live next door to my retreat died a painful death while their conversation—and I use that term lightly—unfolded to its final and furious culmination.

"If your mother was still alive," her father said. Pulling out all the stops and another last-ditch effort of the single parent lost in a sea of bitterness and confusion. Not that I felt sorry for him. The man was a jerk. Had temper issues. Might have been mentally unstable. Still, the loss of a spouse while raising a rebellious child only added to the problem.

"But she's not!" The young woman stomped one white sneaker, arms crossing over her T-shirt, the logo on the front of some kind of cartoon character vanishing behind her forearms. "She's dead, Dad. And I'm done."

So was I, sweetheart. I'd had enough, despite the draw of my inner sense of responsibility, my need to fix others, to help them repair their relationships with one another, to help them heal and move on. This was supposed to be my chance to do all that, to focus on me rather than putting everyone else first.

Except, as I made the choice to back away from the fight and the fence and anything resembling work, the man glanced my way, caught sight of me, and all that ferocious vitriol retargeted itself.

In my direction. Of course, it did.

"Mind your own business!" He took another step down toward his garden, that rage palpable, even from that distance. "Ruining our town isn't good enough for you, tourist? You have to spy on people, too?"

Big inhale, Persephone Pringle. This was no time to lose my temper and there was only one way to ensure I kept control. With a sad little inner sigh for my plans to pamper me and make me the priority, I slipped into the comfortable and familiar role I filled for my clients and allowed the serenity of knowing his anger had nothing to do with me, not really, wash away my animosity while I offered a small smile, not to him, but to the young woman who now stared at me, embarrassment and enough shame to last a lifetime pulling her face down into a sorrowful expression that aged her beyond her young years.

"Persephone," I nodded to her kindly. Her dark gaze widened, flickered to her father in surprise I addressed her, I guess, before she nodded back to me, long, brown ponytail bobbing over one narrow shoulder. "I'm visiting Zephyr for the next few weeks. What a lovely town you have, so picturesque."

"Candace Doiron," the girl said, voice now soft and apologetic, another look for her still vibrating parent more sullen now than angry. "I think you've met my dad, Kendall Doiron." Had I. "Sorry to disturb you." She glared at him then, like this was his fault.

"Not at all," I said. "I happen to be a holistic therapist, and while I'm on vacation, I'd be happy to offer you both my services if you'd like." I held up both hands while the man, to my surprise, remained silent. "Your choice either way. My door is open."

Candace's lips parted, complexion fading to

a more normal tan from the bright pink of her rage, but it was her father who spoke before she could.

"I thought I told you," he said, tone dropped to a deep and abiding fury that came through in every line of his body, in the clenched fists, in his blazing dark eyes, "to mind your own business."

"You could use therapy," Candace snipped.

And that was the end of that, then, wasn't it? Except, as I again decided to retreat and let things simmer down, hoping at least the daughter would take me up on my offer, Mitch appeared at my side, startling me so badly I jumped and meeped out a wee shriek. My host didn't seem to notice, leaning over the top of the fence with enough aggression of his own I had to believe I wasn't the first guest to endure the hateful wrath of the neighbor from hell.

"I've had enough of this, Kendall," Mitch said. "I've warned you about bothering my guests. I'll call the sheriff if I have to." My host, the smiling and somewhat nervous man I'd met just a short time ago had morphed into his own brand of anger. Maybe this town wasn't the adorable photo op I'd imagined, the shiny edges already worn off my enthusiasm.

"Just go ahead and call the sheriff," my neighbor yelled back, his intensity of rage gone again, frankly far more intimidating than the blowhard posturing he engaged in now. The redness had traveled up into his receding hairline, his glasses slipping down his nose until he was forced to shove them back into place with one shaking index finger, the armpits of his golf shirt dark from the lather he'd worked himself into, socks, shorts and dress shoes completing the angry middle-aged man look to perfection.

"I'm so sorry, Persephone," Mitch turned to me, rather red in the face himself, wiping at a sheen of sweat on his upper lip. "I realized I forgot to stock you with towels. I knocked, but when I heard the shouting…" Good to know he didn't just walk in, had some propriety when it came to guest privacy. "I'll make sure he doesn't bother you anymore."

"Kendall!" Oh, dear. I turned to find a dainty and white-haired elderly woman leaning over the other fence, my neighbor on the right throwing her own glove in the ring, it seemed. "You leave this poor young woman alone!"

Mitch's eye roll had me clenching my teeth while attempting to remain optimistic. Because nosy and noisy neighbors hadn't been in the brochure description, had they?

"Stay out of this, you crazy old bat!" How lovely. The delightful neighborhood exchange continued while I seriously considered asking for my deposit back then and there.

"Leave her alone," Mitch shouted.

"You're always causing trouble, Kendall!" The elderly lady wasn't to be outdone, her curly white hair a halo of softness around her wrinkled face, the faded flower pattern of her top making what I could see of her appear washed out by time and the sun, like an ancient, faded blanket left out to the elements.

"Annie, darling," the voice of reason interrupted, an elderly man appearing to tug on her, trying to lead her away from the fray and her shrieking over two fences and my yard to the neighbor who didn't seem to like her, either. "Come now, my darling, it's almost dinner time."

"Oh, do leave off, Henry." She cackled, pale eyes meeting mine. "I'm not done yelling at Kendall."

If ever there was a giant flag waved over a battlefield, I'd just had it tossed to me.

CHAPTER FOUR

Before I could draw Mitch aside and quietly demand my money so I could pack up (thank goodness I hadn't opened my suitcases yet or made any attempt to settle in) and get out of this insane situation while the getting was good, in advance of anything else that could, and likely would, happen, well.

Something else happened.

He strode into Sunshine's backyard like he owned the place, that local law enforcement saunter augmented by the cowboy hat, tan uniform shirt, shiny badge and gun holstered at his hip that, for some reason, gave ordinary men the audacity to feel superior to everyone else. And yes, my biases against men in law enforcement were showing, but I was having a day, it seemed, and the appearance of who had to be the local sheriff—cowboy boots, mustache, slitted and wary eyes and all—only reinforced my decision to exit before my optimism had been completely crushed.

"Kendall's been yelling at Mary again," the old woman piped up as the sheriff came to a halt in front of me.

"That's not Mary, Annie," Henry said, nodding to me. "Apologies for the trouble, ma'am, Mitch, Sheriff Perkins."

"What seems to be the problem, Mitch?" Sheriff Perkins didn't even glance Kendall's way, his gaze instead taking me in like my jean shorts and tank top offended him. Or maybe it was my close-cropped blonde pixie cut, the tattoos I'd been collecting along the way that adorned my upper chest and forearms. I might have been fifty, but I wasn't *old*. Had promised myself old was a word I'd banished from my vocabulary when it came to me and my life and everything that went along with it. Knew my unconventional appearance likely miffed Sheriff Perkins as much as it had embarrassed Trent. Felt my back go up at the judging up and down from the local cop who didn't get to make assumptions about me, assumptions even my ex-husband knew better than to voice.

Barely kept my mouth shut. Like, skin of my teeth, bite my tongue, and any other idiom that fit the bill. Next stop, SnarkBack City.

Mitch, on the other hand, didn't seem to notice the ongoing contempt with which his town's sheriff wielded a disdainful scowl. He was too busy pointing fingers at the neighbors, a truth that didn't detract from the fact I had to stand there and take it when the sheriff visibly wrote me off while Mitch spoke.

"Yet again, Kendall is making trouble for my business and my guests." Mitch's low anger couldn't have reached the other yard, though it didn't keep the now sullenly watchful neighbor from putting in his own two cents.

"This is a family community," Kendall snarled. "I've told the council time and time again it should be illegal to rent the row out. This is our beach, and our home and tourists aren't welcome."

The sheriff finally glanced his way, mustache scrunching as he pursed his lips. "I'm well aware, Kendall. I've had to listen to you argue the point enough times over the years. But in case you forgot that same council keeps denying your demands. That means," he nodded to my host, ignoring me now, "Mitch has every right to rent his cottage to outsiders." At that last word, the sheriff's gaze flickered, side-eye on me. You better believe I got the message, loud and clear. His defense of the council's decision might have said one thing, but it was clear from his partial sneer Perkins was more on Kendall's side of the fence metaphorically than he was Mitch's. Still, apparently, this was a common argument and the sheriff's unhappy arrival wasn't selling the experience very well. "I'm getting really tired of having to come down here, Kendall." That, at least, sounded authentic. "The whole neighborhood is sick of listening to you, so how's about we agree you do your best to keep your opinions on your side of the fence and mind your manners."

That confirmed it *and* my departure. The fact Kendall was a pain in the rear end in general didn't really come as a surprise, but I have to admit the truth hit with devastating disappointment.

I really liked this place.

The sheriff's command had Kendall huffing and puffing, but instead of attempting to blow Perkins down, my neighbor (for now) spun in his black socks and dress shoes with those hideous polyester shorts swishing and went inside, slamming the door behind him.

I'd almost forgotten about the young woman until she spoke up. She'd held so still and stayed out of the conflict between her father and the sheriff, withdrawn sufficiently she'd turned into background, only coming to the forefront again when she spoke.

"Sorry, Sheriff Perkins," Candace's dull apology barely registered above a normal tone of voice, so it took a bit to carry it to us.

"It's not your fault, Candace," Perkins said with a small sigh. He was a human being with some kind of empathy? Amazing. Just reserved for locals, I guess. "Try not to provoke him, okay?"

Her jaw clench had me wondering if she was about to fire off on the sheriff this time. I know I wanted to, not just to defend her. How was her father's blatantly childish behavior her fault and how do tell, did she provoke him, anyway? Of all the misogynistic, male-dominant, arrogant…

Candace kept her composure and, despite my internal turmoil, so did I. "He's worse since Mom died." She shrugged like that wasn't something she could change or deal with. Her eyes met mine, then. "I'll try to keep him out of your hair, Persephone," she said.

Poor thing. "My offer stands." Did it ever. And though I wasn't sure at this point if I could be objective when it came to Kendall, I'd do my very best to give her tools to deal with him. If suggesting she move out was one of those tools? So be it.

Candace nodded but didn't comment further, glaring instead at the back door as she heaved a large and visibly unhappy sigh before heading for the door and disappearing into the house like a soldier on the path to war.

Had me grateful for the excellent relationship I shared with my kid. How she adored her father, and he her. We weren't perfect, we weren't even together anymore. But our love and understanding were real.

I might have been patting myself unnecessarily on the back, but Sheriff Perkins wasn't done with me, whether he was forced to uphold the town's laws or not. He poked an index finger in my direction, thumb of his other hand hooked in his belt loop, that squinting gaze fixed on me as if expecting sass back.

Well, he wasn't wrong.

"Heard about the little incident between you and Kendall at Cherry Tree and Pine Hallow," he said, just enough chastisement in his tone that I remained irritated while trying to figure out what it was he was talking about. Realized he meant Captain Jerkface next door almost hitting me. Except, as Perkins went on it was obvious, he didn't see it my way at all. "Not sure what things are like in the big city, Mrs…?" He looked around as if expecting, what? A husband to show up and manhandle me into compliance?

"Pringle," I said through clenched teeth. "Ms."

He grunted at that, like finding out I was single only reinforced his opinion. My attempt to sink into my therapist calm and poise was already being tested, but this man's attitude had it fading so rapidly I wasn't sure I'd be spending the night in the bed I rented, because if he pushed it any further, I might actually end up in a jail cell for assault.

Temper, temper, missy.

"You just make sure you follow the rules, little lady, and we won't have any issues while you're in our fine town. Will we?" Did he just call me…?

"I think you're done harassing my guest, Sheriff Perkins," Mitch snapped, his own temper rising, though I honestly wished he'd kept his mouth shut because I was already on the brink of making a run for it and the last thing I needed was a man stepping in to manage my business.

I didn't mean to be ungrateful but come on, people.

The sheriff's attention shifted to Mitch. "I'm getting tired of your rentals being a source of tension in our town," he said. "You know better than to make any more trouble, Mitch. Enough folks lost out last year. You're making things harder for the rest of us."

Ah, so this wasn't about me, then, of course, it wasn't. I knew better. This kind of animosity—Kendall's, Candace's, the sheriff's, Mitch, even the old lady over the other fence— all had their own conflicts and I'd wandered into them. It helped a lot, that reminder, diffused a great deal of my animosity and allowed me to put myself into perspective.

"I'm sure everything will work out, Sheriff Perkins," I said, forcing a small smile, though using a professional air rather than a personal one. "I'm only here to vacation in your lovely town, not to have trouble dropped in my lap." No way was I allowing him to make me the bad guy here, regardless of his attitude. "Now, if you'll excuse me, I'd like to talk to my host."

The sheriff hesitated. Since leaving would mean he basically followed my order, it had to rankle. However, after a long and rather uncomfortable moment, he touched the brim of his hat before turning and walking back through the side gate, leaving it wide open while I scowled at that fact.

Was I going to have to deal with strangers strolling through my rental the entire time I was here?

"I'm so sorry, Persephone." Mitch's own temper had faded to a more moderate hum of irritation as he glared after the departing Perkins. "This isn't the norm, I assure you." He must have realized I was going to ask about his refund policy, hands clenching in front of him, eyes a little wide, that prominent Adam's apple of his bobbing away in anxiety. "I'm happy to offer you a discount for your difficulties."

Well, that was nice of him. And, as quiet settled around the property again, both neighbors out of my sight and the soft call of the ocean on the other side of the gate reminding me I had, as yet, to visit the beach, I found myself shrugging in what felt like resignation.

Was I going to let a few crazy neighbors ruin my retreat? Maybe. But, for now, a discount and some privacy sounded like a great idea.

"Thank you, Mitch," I said. "Why don't I take a night and think on it and we'll talk tomorrow?"

He paused just like the sheriff had, though this dismissal was kinder and far more subtle.

"I left the towels on the sofa," he said. "Have a nice evening, Persephone."

The moment he was gone, I exhaled a long sigh, looking up at the blue sky, not quite asking "Why me?" but on the verge.

When a querulous old voice said, "You watch yourself, missy."

CHAPTER FIVE

Surely such a warning should have set me off, considering. The old dear, rather than upsetting me, instead had my curiosity fired up at this point. I crossed to the other side of the yard, closer to her, smiling up at her where she must have been standing on something because the barrier was taller than the one between me and Kendall and unless she had abnormally long legs, she'd found a perch on which to snoop.

Why was I suddenly thinking the fence heights should have been the other way around?

"Thank you for thinking of me, Annie." I chose a kind approach, despite her pinched expression and tone of voice. She softened immediately, both to my attitude and, I hoped, the use of her name that I took from Henry's interaction. "But why do you say that? Am I in trouble?"

She scrunched her nose at me and clung to the top of the fence with both hands, tongue working around in her mouth before she spoke.

"He's been more trouble than usual, Mary," she said, dropping to a whisper they would have heard next door regardless. She wasn't exactly stealthy. "You really need to keep your husband under better control." She brightened then, hopping up and down. That cackle she let out? Had me grinning, despite the fact she clearly mistook me for, who? Kendall's now-deceased wife?

"Annie, dearest," and there was Henry again, popping up next to her, albeit slowly, his energy level nowhere near hers if his laborious heave upward by a firm hold on the pickets meant anything. I was now incredibly curious about the other side of the fence, what they stood on, how they lived. The scent of flowers was stronger here, and not familiar to this garden. It had to be coming over from their side. And the lovely pink of their paint job showing as the top of their house rose over the white pickets stirred the romantic in me, gingerbreading around the eaves an adorable upgrade. "I'm so sorry," he smiled nervously and waved at me before tugging on his wife. "Please, come inside."

Annie lifted one hand free and smacked him, almost casually. I was so surprised by the obvious physical abuse, the sound of the whack, I caught myself staring at Henry, waiting for him to chastise her.

Instead, he accepted it without comment, though his cheeks pinked as he purposely avoided my eyes. Clearly, this was a regular occurrence and something he wasn't proud of. Nor, I would imagine, the flip-flop of her personality from cheerful wickedness to a surge of nasty I didn't envy him.

That woman would be a handful and now I was positive this was the wrong place for me. Crazy on the left and the right? Yes, that word, okay, and I was a therapist. Let me finish. I had enough of my own whacko to deal with to be fielding flanking crackpots on my vacation time.

Annie seemed to forget immediately that Henry had interrupted her. She waggled her rather impressively bushy eyebrows at me with a giggle that ended in a snorting grunt before huffing her way down, her chatter muffled behind the wooden boards. I stayed put and listened to the two until the sound of their door closing wrapped me in the soft silence of my own garden again.

No, Mitch's garden. The backyard of nutso crankypants yelling and shouting people. The retreat into madness, not tranquility. Darn it. I really, really liked it here.

Stood there for a long moment, agonizing over my next move. I could have just left. Was fairly certain Mitch would cave and let me have my deposit back. I could hit the road, get a cheap hotel, spend the evening looking for a new rental. Right, because finding a place on the beach for four weeks uninterrupted in Maine in summer was going to be a piece of cake. I might as well have asked for a holy miracle. I'd booked this trip months in advance on purpose, knowing what the tourism season was like. I'd be lucky to get a decent hotel that didn't cater to by-the-hour guests.

Which had me looking around, sour and disgruntled. No, disenchanted. My happy little fantasy had turned into a nightmare.

Then again, was I overreacting? Had I simply had a bad start that would turn into a truly lovely stay? As I looked around, even the creepy gnomes seemed happy to have me there. And it was getting later, already almost 6:30PM. I debated one last moment, then made a choice.

One night, as I'd told my host. We'd see how things went and then I'd decide. If the fighting continued to interrupt my retreat, I'd consider other options. For now, however, I was going to make the best of the space and try to forget the events of the last little bit.

The crack of the seal on the fresh bottle of lemon gin made me smile, glug of the container decanting a generous amount into a short tumbler, mint and a squirt of cranberry and a lot of ice from the new bag Mitch left in the freezer music to my ears. The first sip tasted so divine I did a little dance in the kitchen, pulling out my phone and the playlist I'd created for gin and making dinner and having a personal party soon elevating my mood, broadcast through my sound pebble to amplify it enough to fill the room without making the neighbors mad.

Why I cared, on the other hand. But my mother raised me to be polite to strangers, so I did as I was taught despite the fact it had been a very long time since I let her tell me what to do.

To my delight, I didn't have to go out to get ingredients for dinner, a dainty casserole dish with some chicken something prepped and waiting in the fridge, along with a small loaf of what looked like homemade garlic bread and a note attached a welcome from Mitch that had me thinking much kindlier toward the man. Since I happened to be a crap cook, it was a good thing he included the oven instructions, but it wasn't long before the scent of garlic, onion and melting cheese filled the small space, my second gin already gone by the time the twenty minutes were up.

I carried my plate and third drink—who was counting?—out to the sunroom, the sky still light, screens letting in a breeze when I wound the glass open to expose the flowers and lane and quiet of the evening to surround me.

While I tended to avoid pasta—that last twenty pounds resisted every diet I tried, though I suppose gin didn't help—let alone bread, the indulgence paired with two drinks had me happy and full and contented as I sat back to sip at the remains of my cocktail to wait for sunset.

"I can't take this anymore!" Candace stormed out the front of their cottage, my open windows not only allowing her shouting to reach me but offering a clear line of sight as she headed down their path toward the small wooden gate and a light blue scooter, helmet in her hands.

"Just go then!" Kendall yelled after her,

front door slamming behind her, though she was already well on her way to the road.

If I hadn't been drinking, I'm positive I would have stayed very still and out of sight and tried to avoid Candace. I had this thing, however, when it came to gin. Some women claimed it made them more friendly toward the opposite sex. Me? Turned me into a nosy and overly helpful busybody.

I was on the move and out the side door, calling her name before she could reach the street and I could think better of butting in. Candace looked up, tears on her cheeks, the poor thing in a state that told me they'd likely been fighting since she went back inside.

"Are you okay?" I'd brought my drink out with me, knew the clinking ice told its own story, hoped I didn't sound like I'd had three already. "Did you need to talk?"

She stopped, looked like she might take me up on it. Then shook her head, closing the distance to her scooter and jamming the helmet over her dark hair.

"You can't help me," she said, climbing on board. Her eyes lifted to mine, more sorrow than anger there. "But thank you. I might take you up on it later when I calm down." She drove off then, the hum of the electric motor the only sound, disappearing long before she did at the corner of the lane, heading for town and whatever solace she could find there.

I found myself glaring at the house next door, the ordinary beige paint with black trim an oddity for the colorful street, some kind of nose-thumbing on Kendall's part, no doubt, to the cutesy image the others tried to create. At least he was the last in line and didn't stick out like a sore thumb unless one came down this far.

Kendall chose that moment to emerge, stomping toward the end of the lane. Caught sight of me while I scowled back and spoke up, as I was wont to do.

"You're driving her away, you know," I said.

"For the last time," he shouted at me, "and I won't tell you again--mind your own business! Or else!" Whatever his reason for being in the yard, he clearly forgot about it because he about-faced and went back inside, another shattering door slam likely a terror on his hinges.

Fine. Business minded. I saluted him with the remains of my gin and went inside for another.

CHAPTER SIX

By the time the sun set, a rather unremarkable event that had me sighing at the letdown and heading to the garden with a shrug, it was already 8:20PM. I had a bit of a worry about mosquitoes, reminded I'd forgotten to bring spray, but hoped I'd get to enjoy the backyard for a bit and not be driven inside by the pests and my lack of foresight.

As I passed through the kitchen and onto the deck, turning on the light as I went, I had the second of what I hoped wasn't a series of starts that had me clutching at my heart and spilling some of my drink while gasping loudly enough to send the small, old woman at the foot of the stairs spinning to look up at me. Annie still wore the faded flower pattern, though it was now revealed to be a dress, thin body draped in a light pink sweater over the worn fabric, her feet bare and covered in sand. But it was the garden gnome she clutched in her hands that had my attention the most, her guilty expression turning to accusation in a heartbeat, both hands holding him tightly around the neck.

"He's mine," she said, tucking the ugly thing against her narrow chest, snuggling it almost like a baby. When she looked down at it and cooed, the action had me wondering, sad for her all over again. Was she missing an infant she raised and saw grow up to leave her? A child she lost? Or the ghost of one she never got to hold?

It didn't matter and I wasn't so heartless as to ask. Instead, I slowly approached, smiling and open so she wouldn't tumble further into upset, gesturing at the statue in her possession.

"He's adorable," I smiled back. "What's his name?"

That question changed everything. Annie lit up like a fireworks display, now coy and giggling, looking down with bright eyes at the surrogate to whatever past she was lost in. "Lewis," she whispered. She held the thing out toward me then, for my admiration, which I gave to the best of my ability before she tucked it away once more, under the lip of her sweater, rocking side to side with it while she hummed. "Lewis," she repeated. Sighed deeply. The saddest sigh I'd ever heard.

Hard not to feel sorry for her. Or to step aside and give her what made her happy in the moment, even if only for that moment, until reality or some other memory jumble interfered. Mitch could deal with the old lady as he saw fit, but I wasn't about to start anything else, thanks. Besides, it was impossible not to feel empathy, especially when I didn't have a horse in this race.

Let her take it home. I couldn't care less if the silly thing ended up in her yard or not. Actually, I would prefer it so we'd both be happy.

Her pale eyes widened before she grinned at me like a little kid caught with something she wasn't supposed to have only to be granted permission to have it. "All three are mine," she said then, greed a living thing flashing over her face, the baby reference forgotten, statue again held by the neck, her body turning away from me to protect it just in case I tried to take it away.

Was that the game, though? Did she want me to try? I never got the chance to find out.

"Annie? Annie!" Henry's voice carried, from their side of the fence.

"In here, Henry," I said, sitting on the top step while the sound of someone circling the perimeter ended in the elderly man coming through the partially open gate, his relief at finding Annie in my yard mixed firmly with embarrassment. He hurried forward as quickly as he could, though he seemed to struggle with mobility, while Annie danced away from his grasping hands, her ability to move not restricted by age.

"Mine!" She stuck her tongue out at him. "She said I could."

Regardless of my generosity, Henry finally caught her and liberated the gnome, setting it down and shooting me an apologetic look. "Come home, dear," he said. "It's bedtime and you need your pills."

Annie pouted but did as she was told, looking back at me with an intense stare that didn't break until they exited the gate and disappeared from view. I heard them talking, his low, urgent tone, her more high-pitched protest, that ended when their door closed. Sighed into the evening air, sipped my gin, noted the lack of biting insects and shrugged.

That was one good thing, right? Because I now debated which neighbor was going to be more of an irritant, the shouty, mean one or the old lady with a penchant for larceny.

I was about to rise, the fallen gnome begging for attention I refused to give, when something glowing caught my attention, freezing me in place. I settled once more as a large, white cat with the fluffiest fur I'd ever seen strolled out of the garden, her green eyes no longer reflecting the light in that creepy way, impressive tail forming a question mark over her back when she paused to look up at me.

"I'm Persephone," I said, noting the bell and small metal charm on her pink collar, though she was too far from me to tell what it said. "Nice meeting you, neighbor."

She mewed softly, inquisitive, sitting in the small patch of grass, ears perked. Which sent me to the kitchen for a piece of chicken from dinner, hoping she hadn't disappeared. Instead of leaving, she'd come closer, now seated primly with that fluff of a tail wrapped around her paws, waiting for me. As if expecting me to serve her, the princess.

Which I did, offering a chunk of the chicken to her, wanting to pet her but worried she'd run off. She sniffed delicately at the offering before looking up and into my eyes again.

Giving me a view of the tag attached to her collar. "Belladonna," I said, keeping my voice low, reaching out to stroke her cheek. "What a beautiful name for a beautiful kitty."

She leaned briefly into the caress then stood, flicking her tail before dashing off into the garden and out the gate to the beach. I hugged my knees, wishing she'd stayed, not sure why I felt lonely all of a sudden. Silly to feel that way when this was exactly what I'd wanted, right?

I took a moment to fulfill a task I'd planned on, dragging the lawn lounger out the gate to the beach, standing a moment to admire the moon rising over the quietly undulating water, the Atlantic Ocean's cold waves lapping at the white sand in welcome. Not the best swimmer, I hoped to get some time in when the tide was lower and the tidal pools warmed by the sun, content to observe its inky darkness for now.

Tired suddenly and ready for bed, I headed inside, latching both the beach and side gates behind me, before locking both doors and settling in to sleep away this very odd day.

***

The crash that woke me from a dead sleep had me lurching upward, clutching at the thin blanket, heart pounding, though groggily wondering if I'd been dreaming or if the sound I'd heard happened in the real world.

When nothing else happened, no other loud noises followed, I half-convinced myself I had a nightmare, lying there long enough to get my pulse under control before sighing and heaving myself out of bed to check, just in case.

My silk kimono served to protect me from prying eyes as I exited the bedroom and headed through the dark living room, checking the sunroom, lit by the corner streetlight sufficiently to prove nothing untoward had happened there. It wasn't until I entered the kitchen, toe hitting something that skittered over the hardwood floor, I realized the sound had been real after all.

When I switched on the light, I was grateful I'd only kicked the shard of glass, not stepped on it fully, the shattered window to the back garden in shining pieces all over the floor.

I quickly retreated to the bedroom and retrieved my sandals, hurrying back to the kitchen and out the door, looking for the culprit. Noted the back gate to the beach was open again if just a little. I knew I'd latched it, made a conscious effort to do so, and fought off a little rush of fear someone chose to circumvent the clearly inadequate safety precautions. Thought of Mitch, thought of Trent and his FBI worst-case scenarios he always used to make me feel afraid. And shoved away the urge to hide in the bathroom until morning.

I was a grown woman who could take care of herself, and I would do so, imaginary or real serial killers notwithstanding.

My steps firmly carried me to the gate, though I admit some trepidation when I poked my head out. Saw nothing, no one and slammed it closed, setting the latch again. Looked up, realized how easy it would be to reach over if one was of a certain height—I doubted I could manage it without assistance, but a taller person wouldn't have a problem— and undo the simple hook. Especially if one was familiar with the placement of that hook, like a neighbor, maybe? While I thought of Annie originally, she was shorter than I was. Which left a cranky next-door problem as the most likely culprit.

I shoved that aside for now and headed back for the stairs and the house, looking up at movement, catching sight of Annie in the second-floor window, staring down at me.

Shivered at the intensity of her attention, until the light went out.

I retrieved a broom from the hall closet after a short search and proceeded to sweep up the glass, only then realizing what caused the damage.

A rock, perfectly round and gray, had been thrown through the pane and when I flipped it over, realized it was more than a projectile. It was a message, scrawled in thick, black marker.

GO HOME.

Earlier tonight, that might have been enough to send me scurrying. Now?

The only way I was leaving was as a cold, dead body.

CHAPTER SEVEN

I sat in the kitchen with the rock on the table, now tucked into a zipper bag, glass disposed of in the trash, temper a wickedly rollicking rollercoaster of emotional turmoil composed of trying to talk myself down while knowing exactly who threw the stupid thing through my window and purposely scared the crap out of me at two in the morning because he was a jerkcicle jerky jerkherder.

You better believe I was planning to call the sheriff in the morning and point fingers right at Mr. Not-So-Neighborly Jerkfacebro Kendall Meaniepants while demanding Mitch not just give me my money back but pay *me* for emotional wear and tear and general distress. This was not going to end well for any of the parties even remotely involved in this entire disastrous and offensive action and I would be not just putting Zephyr in my rearview at the earliest convenience, I'd be leaving a scathing review of Sunshine Cottage and the town in general.

And yes, I was well aware I'd only just a short time ago professed my cold, dead body intent, so apparently, my temper liked waffling. Hissy fit well underway, I'd still managed to maintain a little composure, enough to think things through before doing something I might regret. Like marching over to Kendall's house and handing him his rock back. We'd see how *he* liked it. Or, more importantly, messing up evidence of his guilt (oh, he was guilty, make no mistake) by handling the rock with my bare skin.

And while I had no idea if they could fingerprint stone, I'd done my due diligence (Trent or no Trent, I'd watched enough crime shows to take some precautions despite knowing they were mostly made up but based in truth, right?) just in case the item in question could put an end to the terrible ordeal, not just for me, either. If Kendall went to jail for being an all-around asshat, maybe Candace would find some peace.

I was seriously starting to hate this place and that wasn't an emotion I appreciated being forced into when I was supposed to be on vacation getting all Zen and centered and mentally healthy.

I finally went back to bed, headache looming from the lack of sleep and, admittedly, a little more gin than had been warranted for a night in alone if one wanted to point fingers and make judgments about such things. After forcing down a giant glass of water and two painkillers just in case, I tucked under the covers and, despite the upset and lingering ax murderer scenarios that tried to take over, I fell back to sleep fairly quickly.

The stupid, bright and intrusively cheery sun woke me, curtains pulled but only the flimsy gauze, not the full panels that should have been in place if my host really cared even a little about the comfort of his guests. I groaned and swore a little and moped in grumpy crankiness a full minute before sighing out my temper tantrum and taking responsibility. It had been my forgetfulness, my fault I didn't get to sleep in as I'd hoped and instead dragged my sorry butt all the way (like, five steps) to the bathroom and a shower before making that call.

Which I didn't get to make, not right away, munching a little breakfast cereal and sipping a cup of coffee (Mitch, at least, thought of my creature comforts, if only as a clear indication he expected trouble) when someone called me first. The contact came in via social media, and only one person I knew had become addicted to that mode of communication, so I had to get a grip on myself before I answered because my first instinct was to tell her everything and that just wouldn't do.

This trip had been my idea, was supposed to be awesome. I was not telling my daughter I'd screwed up, made a mistake, was likely coming home that very day. She didn't need to worry about me until after I was back in Wallace and there was nothing more she could do about it.

Manipulating my kid? You better believe it. For both our sakes.

"Callie," I said when I answered the video chat, forcing some cheer into my tone. "Morning, sweetie."

"Hey, Mom!" Her perkiness helped somewhat, though I was sure I looked a fright on the other end of the picture. She turned her head after saying hello, head of thick, dark curls caught in a ponytail that did nothing to tame them before she turned back to me, hazel eyes bright, freckles across her nose shifting as she wrinkled it at me. "How was your first night?"

Under normal circumstances? I would have

teased her with nothing untoward to tell. Wanted to, had to stop and think about it. Was it my hesitation that alerted her? Probably. I'd never been able to lie to her, not since she was little. For some reason, she could read me like yesterday's newspaper. Whatever the case, her cheeriness faded to worry as she leaned in, dimples disappearing, full lips pursing.

"Oh my god," she said. "What happened?"

She was as nosy as I was. "I'm fine," I said. And winced as I realized professing my present condition that way preambled the fact I previously hadn't enjoyed that state of fineness. "Everything's fine." I really needed to stop using that word. "I'm okay, I promise."

Could I have dug myself a deeper hole? Apparently not, my daughter's instant concern increasing with every word until she was wide-eyed and shaking her head.

"Mom," she said in that accusing tone she used with me since I told her about the divorce, like I was the daughter and she the mother. "What happened?"

How did she make that question sound like I'd done something wrong? Meanwhile, I was leaping to conclusions and maybe feeling a little like it was my fault since I'd come here of my own choosing.

"You remember that guy yelling at me

yesterday?" I watched her nod quickly, breath bated, gaze wide and waiting. "He lives next door." I hadn't meant to deliver that in so dry a fashion, but it made her gasp and then giggle, hands covering her mouth, thick lashes fluttering around her large eyes.

"Mom, that's awful," she said. "Is he a total jerk?"

"You wouldn't believe it," I said. "And the other side? A crazy old lady who's into garden gnomes." And breaking into my yard. Sigh.

"Are you going to stay?" Calliope's opinion on that choice came through loud and clear. "Mom, you should leave."

The thing was, hadn't I just been thinking the exact same thing? That this was a terrible choice after all, and I was going to call Mitch and the sheriff and skedaddle? So why then did I suddenly dig in my heels when my daughter mentioned it?

Pride, Persephone Pringle. Ridiculous, foolish pride, that's why.

"I'll work it out," I said. "I'll call the sheriff this morning and he'll handle it."

That had Calliope even more worked up. And, to my sudden groan of horror, I realized she wasn't alone, was she?

Trent was there and heard every word. Popped his head into the video feed, frowning at me with that FBI agent's stern glare of disapproval, almost shoving our daughter out of the way to pounce.

Like he'd been waiting for a reason.

"Why do you need the sheriff?" Trent's own dark curls had been cut so short they barely made waves, his golfer's tan deepening the lines around his eyes and stern mouth, hazel eyes that matched Calliope's narrowed under heavy brows that made him look like a stern and bossy professor, not a decorated law enforcement agent.

She could have warned me. Irritated all over again, I filled them both in on the full events of the previous afternoon and evening, shared the rock through the window story, and even showed Trent—when he insisted—the weapon through the plastic bag.

"This is serious, Seph," my ex-husband said. Like I didn't know that already. "Do you want me to call for you?"

I'd rather he smothered me with a pillow. Inhaled slowly, knowing in my heart he was just trying to help. Wanted to protect me still, regardless of our marital status. To be the hero. My hero.

While I chose to be my own shero.

"I've got it handled," I said. "The guy is harmless, I swear. If he really wanted to hurt me, he'd have done more than throw a rock. That's a coward's weapon, Trent, and you know it." He paused, nodded. "I'll call the sheriff right now and have him take care of things. You two have a great day and I'll be in touch." I hung up rather abruptly, wishing I hadn't had this conversation at all.

It only served to remind me there would always be ties to the life I used to live I just couldn't shake, no matter how many retreats I took or attempts I made to be my own person. Not that it was a horrible thing to be Calliope's mom, to the contrary. I adored my kid. Nor being Trent's former spouse. As I said, he was a good person, a truly kind man with a genuine love for what he did, for solving crimes and making the world a safer and better place.

I was just tired of the part I'd come to play in their lives. Escaping that scenario, it seemed, even for a little while, wasn't solving anything. I glared at the rock for a moment before setting it aside with a small thank you to it, to Kendall. Ah-ha moments came at the oddest times but if you were ready for them? Solved a lot of old hurts.

I didn't need a retreat. I needed to find new ways to be me without falling back into who I hated being.

My next call wasn't to the sheriff, however.

Mitch answered a moment after the first ring, cheery, "Good morning, Persephone!" about to have the wind knocked out of it.

His obvious horror at the incident came through in a rush of words. "I'm so sorry, I'll go talk to him right away, I'll deal with this personally, are you all right?"

I hung up from him after assuring him I was, and, with a sigh, finally called what amounted to law enforcement in Zephyr, Maine.

Got the receptionist who put me through to the sheriff's voicemail. "You've reached Thomas Perkins, leave a message."

Mine was quick and to the point, followed by my phone number. I hung up, leaning back in the kitchen chair, suddenly restless. Surged to my feet, tossed my phone aside and headed for the garden and the back gate and the beach, the glorious, glorious beach.

CHAPTER EIGHT

The tide had come in, risen high, almost to the edge of the sand, thin strip beckoning me like a pathway to oblivion as the stretch of shoreline ran off into the distance. I walked it in bare feet, hands in my pockets, breathing deeply and making choices I should have made before I took this ridiculous trip, though knowing I wouldn't have come to the ones I now made without the smack in the butt the Universe just handed to me.

I'd sit down with Trent and Calliope, separately and then together, and we would redefine our relationships to one another out loud. Why hadn't I done so before? It was time to collaborate on our futures, instead of skidding sideways and trying to compromise, to face this new way of being head-on and with optimism instead of fear of making waves or things worse. I knew better. I taught my clients these things, walked so many families through the navigation of their own private minefields of blame, shame and grief. I had to admit it, I wasn't infallible, far from it. And sometimes seeing trees for the forest or the other way around came hard for even the most knowledgeable of us.

I had to be honest with myself. Was harder for those of us who knew better. Like every other profession, we fell short when it came time for the hidden darkness and shadows of doubt we carried to come into the light and be released. I didn't know a single therapist who wouldn't agree that our kind were the ones who needed therapy the most.

The deepest irony of being a helping hand to strangers was how hard it became to offer that same gesture to those I loved. Not to mention myself. And while this retreat had been meant for that purpose, I couldn't get past the feeling maybe—just maybe—I hadn't left Wallace and Calliope and Trent and my friends, my mom, everyone, just to find myself.

I'd run away because I didn't know how to be with them any more than they knew how to be with me now that circumstances had changed so drastically.

Okay, sure, I'd been out of the house a while, out of my marriage a year before the papers were officially signed. But something about the finality, wanted or not, freeing and liberating or not, still carried a weight I'd been refusing to acknowledge.

Why? Because I didn't want to admit I failed? Surely, I wasn't that shallow. And nor was it regret for all the time I'd "wasted" because I hated that reference. Trent and I had a few good years, a brilliant and beautiful kid and a friendship that I hoped would last. And I was still young, right?

Grief. I'd come here to grieve. So, it was time I got to it and finally accepted the death of the old along with the bright shiny of the new. Because until I did, that new would only get tarnished, fade in luster and lose its joy. No way was I allowing this chance to be who I always knew I could be to pass me by because I was too stubborn to embrace all of it.

Sunlight shone on the glassy water, the barest waves washing toward shore, my toes wet from the sand, soul lighter than it had been in a very long time. I turned back toward my cottage after about a half hour or so, meandering my way on the return, feeling much better. The tide retreated as I strolled, giving me more beach to play with as I examined seashells and tossed small pebbles into the water.

While planning to leave Zephyr, taking a slow and roundabout drive home via a few stops in cute little towns along the way for a couple of overnights before going home and getting back to the job of being Calliope's mom, Trent's ex-wife, my client's support and my own person.

It wasn't until I was almost back, I realized there was something in the water I hadn't noticed before. I paused, squinting at the floating, bobbing object. The beach was devoid of driftwood, though whether because nothing washed up here typically or due to a cleanup effort by the town, I wasn't sure, but the way it moved had me pausing to study it, head tilting, squinting as the morning sun cast a glare on the water that made it hard to distinguish details.

I'm still not sure what impulse had me splashing my way out to check, what awful weight woke inside me, dread clutching at my stomach, my chest, or exactly when I realized what I was looking at. All I remembered was sloshing the last few steps to the mass in the water, a pair of dress shoes and dark socks aimed in my direction.

My hand guided the thing in a slow circle, waves lifting, lapping and undulating its—his,

Persephone, *his*—body, arms outstretched, golf shirt dark with moisture, face staring upward, exposed to the sunlight, brown eyes filmed over with white and water-filled mouth agape. Kendall Doiron had yelled at me—at anyone—for the last time.

Death appeared to be a more powerful motivator than a rock through my window because when I rushed home to call the sheriff, he phoned me back immediately.

"I'm on my way," he huffed on the other end of the line, the sound of a car door slamming proof of his words. "Don't touch anything."

The fact I'd already dragged Kendall's body onto the sand so it wouldn't float away? I'd keep that little detail to myself, then, wouldn't I? I hurried back to the scene to ensure no one tampered with the corpse, the sun already drying his clothing, leaving behind white patches of salt. While it was only a matter of minutes before Sheriff Perkins arrived, I had time to do a cursory examination of the body—from a distance, I promise. Since this wasn't my first corpse, I didn't have the squeamish reaction I'd endured last time, surprised at how easy it was to compartmentalize the man's death and focus on the more important matter of whether this was, in fact, foul play or some kind of accident.

Or maybe Kendall Doiron had walked into the ocean and let it do its work? Though the man didn't seem the type to put everyone in his life out of misery, let alone his own. Too ornery. And yes, I was thinking ill of the dead because he'd given me no reason to do otherwise.

I never understood people's need to glorify the deceased when the fact was the man had been a jerk and death didn't change that one little bit.

From what I could tell, there seemed to be a rather large dent in the side of his skull that more than likely was the cause of his present state, though I held off getting any closer, a fact I deemed the right choice when the sound of footfalls and huffing approached me at a rapid speed. I turned to find Sheriff Perkins and two deputies running toward me, the sheriff stopping at my side with red cheeks and struggling for breath while his more youthful sidekicks appeared none the worse for wear.

"You found him like this?" Perkins managed to get that out, chest heaving a little while he waved for his deputies to get to work. Which they did, using yellow tape and wooden pickets they'd brought with them to cordon off the area. Seemed a little silly to me, but it wasn't my crime scene.

"I found him in the water," I said, fessing up to the truth, gesturing at the retreating tide. "I was worried the waves would carry him out, so I dragged him to the beach."

Perkins scowled, though he couldn't fault my logic, could he? "Step back, Ms. Pringle," he said. "But don't go anywhere. I'll have questions for you in a moment."

I did as I was told despite the gnawing irritation at his treatment, the fact he didn't thank me or make any acknowledgment whatsoever that if I hadn't acted the body would be gone and no one would know what happened to Kendall Doiron.

As I stepped over the yellow line one of the deputies lowered for me before tying it securely and carrying on, the sound of someone calling had my empathy stirring at last. I caught Candace before she could run through the tape, held her back while the sheriff and his boys ignored her, the young woman collapsing against me at the sight of her father on the sand.

"Is he…?" She gulped then sobbed once

before stilling. "This is just horrible. What happened?"

"I'm sure the sheriff will have more information for you shortly," I said, turning her gently away to face the water.

Candace met my eyes, hers full of tears but the full-on weep fest I'd expected not coming. Sure, they'd had their conflicts. Still, her lack of overwhelmed grief felt odd to me. Then again, this was the second parent she'd lost in a year, so perhaps she was simply in shock.

"You found him?" I nodded at her question. "Did he drown?"

I didn't answer that. "Can I make you a cup of coffee? We can wait for the sheriff at your house." We were only a stone's throw from her garden gate, my own just past. I glanced up at the sight of movement, a few neighbors further down the beach drawn to the arrival of the sheriff, no doubt. And, among the gawkers, Annie and Henry, though while he looked worried, she seemed amused.

A short, round man, face covered in sweat he mopped with a white handkerchief, hustled down the beach toward us, a black case in one hand, his bowtie askew and bald head shining in the sunlight. He nodded to both of us as he drew parallel, stopping to grasp Candace's hand.

"I'm so sorry, my dear," he said in a lovely soft tenor, light blue eyes meeting mine under bushy brows, round face red from the heat and effort, but kindly. "You found the body?"

"Persephone Pringle," I said, offering my hand.

"Lou Savoy," he said. "I'm the funeral home director, but I second as town coroner." He tsked softly, that gentle sweetness aimed at Candace again. "When I heard it was your dad… my dear, if there's anything Linda and I can do for you?"

"Lou!" The sheriff barked the man's name, the coroner sighing.

"I suppose business first," he said, nodding to me. "Please, take care of Candace. She's been through so much." He patted her shoulder while she stood there, mute and still. "I'll have Linda drop in on you later, my girl, if that's okay?"

She bobbed a little nod and while I was certain it wasn't an enthusiastic agreement to the plan, more of an absent acceptance just to get him to go, he took it at face value and continued on his way, thanking the deputy who let him through with a rather jovial good nature I had originally anticipated from a small town like this. At least someone in Zephyr wasn't a total asshat.

CHAPTER NINE

The sheriff joined us almost immediately, scowling over his notepad as he squared off like he was about to do battle instead of ask me questions. Had my back up with that attitude, you better believe it, and contemplated demanding a lawyer just in case. Despite not needing one because I didn't kill the dude next door.

Might have thought about it briefly but thinking and doing weren't even close.

"You said Mr. Doiron threw a rock through your window last night." The sheriff just put words in my mouth and now I really was on the verge of lawyering up. Instead of snapping in response, however, or insisting I said no such thing, I hugged Candace against me when she made a soft sound of protest.

"If you listen to my message again, Sheriff Perkins," I said a little more firmly than I intended but firm appeared to be the only tone he heard, "I made no such accusation. Only that an unknown someone decided to vandalize the cottage with a distinct message written on the rock." Wait, had I accused Kendall? Now Perkins had me doubting myself, second-guessing the rapid-fire voicemail I'd left. I tried a mental scan, knew my memory wasn't going to suffice and gritted my teeth against the possibility maybe I had said something of that nature.

Perkins didn't argue the context, so I must have been right. Trusting my instincts had never been something I questioned, and suddenly this place had me kerfuffled? No more doubt. I couldn't afford it, not in this circumstance and, you know what? Not ever.

The sheriff squinted at me, lips thinned out under his bushy mustache. "Go home," he said. "That was the message, correct?"

I nodded. "I have the rock in question preserved in plastic and waiting for your examination." Let him try to challenge that. I wasn't expecting Candace to pull gently away from me, shaking her head, though not in denial but guilt and shame.

"I wouldn't put that past Dad,

Persephone," she said, hugging herself, as if cutting off and denying any possible support or comfort, shivering despite the warmth of the morning. Definitely in shock and in need of either a hospital visit or at the very least a long sleep and a chance to grieve. "He's been known to vandalize before."

I wished I'd known that before I found his dead body. Heck, before I trusted Mitch's pretty pictures on the internet, his compelling write-up about Sunshine Cottage and Zephyr. Before I'd leaped into this mess without a second thought. "Whatever the case," I said, "while I was upset by the early hour wake-up call, I held off my own judgments until I could speak to you, Sheriff Perkins." So there. Yeah, a big, fat lie, but he didn't have to know that and neither did Candace. The poor girl was suffering enough, and I didn't need to add my judgment to her hurt. Wouldn't. "Despite his animosity, I wasn't about to jump to any conclusions." And now wondered if it had been him or was he dead here on the beach long before the vandalism? Had he died shortly after? No way for me to tell, but perhaps the coroner would be able to identify the time of death.

None of my business but didn't stop my mind from leaping to questions over possibilities and around likelihoods into the realm of poking my nose in where it didn't belong.

"You sure about that?" The sheriff didn't seem convinced, still squinting, still scowling. "You sure you didn't catch him in the act and lose that temper of yours, Ms. Pringle? Hit him over the head?"

Now, this was just getting ridiculous. "Right," I said, that temper he mentioned showing up in cynical sarcasm, "that's why I phoned in the vandalism instead of trying to hide it so I wouldn't look guilty." Paused. "So, it was foul play. He was struck with something?"

Perkins's narrowed gaze tightened until I could barely see his pupils. "That's not important," he said.

"It certainly is," I said. "If you're accusing me of something, I'll be requesting legal counsel. My ex-husband is an FBI agent, Sheriff Perkins, and this isn't my first murder investigation. I know my rights."

I might as well have confessed to killing Kendall Doiron. The sheriff immediately perked, jaw jumping.

"You've been a murder suspect before, have you?" He wrote that down while I realized my mistake and spluttered, Candace's creased and anxious expression not helping even a little to regain my composure.

"Not a suspect," I said. "I investigated and uncovered the murderer."

That had Perkins even more in a tizzy, a vein in his forehead standing out, mustache wriggling in an undulating dance. Whatever it was he planned to say, however, didn't come out before my phone rang, interrupting his train of accusation. I turned slightly away from him, my own jaw clenching at the number but knowing if I didn't pick up, he'd call me over and over again until I did. Or, worse yet, drive all the way up here and get involved. It was like him to follow up, to nag me about calling the sheriff. I just had to hold it together long enough to get him off the phone without alerting him to the fact a lot more happened since the rock through the window.

The last thing I needed was my ex-husband poking his FBI agent nose in this mess.

"Trent," I said. "Can I call you back?"

"There's been a murder?" Wait, how did he know that? And so much for keeping him out of it. "Seph, are you okay?"

Oh, for goodness' sake. "I'm fine." Yikes, there was that word again. "I'll call you later."

"Your name was mentioned in the case report," he said. Which meant he'd been keeping an eye on me, which had my hackles raised and my anger bubbling and all kinds of resentment waking up and waving flags of protest. "Did you find the body? Seph, was it the next-door neighbor you had trouble with? Tell me you didn't do something stupid."

Did he actually just suggest…?

"If you come here," I snarled into the phone with more heat than the summer sun, "I swear to God, Trent Garret, I will never, ever speak to you again. Do you understand me?"

His long, empty silence held until I caught my breath. "I just want to help."

"The local police can handle it." And there was the guilt at overreacting, though I *wasn't* overreacting. I wasn't his to worry about anymore. "If I run into any issues, I'll call. And stop spying on me." I hung up, a bit harsh, I know. But better than the alternative that would have been a messy meltdown in front of both the grieving daughter of the victim and the judging sheriff.

"You were saying," I addressed Perkins rather primly.

My phone rang for a second time. He stared pointedly at it while I heaved a quick, annoyed sigh and did my pivot again, this time answering with a soft, "I'm okay, Callie. I can't talk right now."

"Mom." When did she start taking on her father's tone of voice? "Dad's really worried and so am I. You need to come home right now."

"I can't leave until I give my statement," I said. Felt my insides crumble, my resolve from the walk earlier dissolve as disappointment and frustration won, turning to doubt. "But you're right, this isn't working out. I'll let you know when I'm on the road."

"I love you, Mom," Calliope said, sounding more herself.

Why did my acquiescence mean she got to go back to normal while I fell into regret and dull compliance? "Love you too, sweetheart." When I hung up this time it was with a heavy heart and a distinct flavor of failure in my mouth.

I wasn't used to failing, so it stung, let me tell you.

"Ms. Pringle," the sheriff interrupted my moment of weakness with a definitively snarly tone, "you're not going anywhere." It would have been so easy to snap back, to let my snarky side win out. Instead, I held it firmly in check while he slapped the cover of his leather notebook closed and shoved it into his back pocket. "You're not to leave town for any reason," he went on, "until I'm satisfied my investigation is complete. Are we clear?"

I nodded, temper in check, but barely. "I assure you, I had nothing to do with Kendall's murder."

"I'll be the judge of that," he said. "But as of right now, Ms. Pringle, you're my prime suspect."

My ability to stay quiet met an untimely end as did my restraint. "You have got to be kidding me," I shot back. "The man was a menace. There had to be any number of people who wanted him dead."

Candace let out a soft moan that ended in a sob. I really stepped in it this time, anger falling away, reaching for her in compassion only to have her run from us, heading toward her gate, disappearing through it while the sheriff glared.

"I thought you were some kind of therapist," he grunted.

Snarl.

"Sheriff!" He spun, one of his deputies approaching with a familiar object in a large plastic bag, his gloved hands cradling the garden gnome doing nothing to hide the hair and blood sticking to its pointed hat. "I think we found the murder weapon."

Well, that was craptastic. Because unless I was mistaken, wasn't that from my rented garden? Then again, there had to be millions of the ugly things around the country, right? I wracked my brain, trying to remember if one was missing, couldn't recall, turned to find Annie and Henry had gone. Wait, she took one, didn't she?

No, he'd made her put it back.

Tell me it wasn't one of mine.

CHAPTER TEN

"Look familiar, Ms. Pringle?" My hope the sheriff didn't know about the gnomes Mitch kept in the garden ended up dashed to bits with that question. "Let's go take a look and be sure, shall we?" He gestured for me to precede him, the statue in question still held in one hand. It took me a moment to realize what he wanted, but his pointed glance at the garden gate and impatient stare finally had me clue in.

Which meant I found myself marching back to the rental property, through the back fence and to the deck, dread growing with every step, my eyes roving the ground the moment the stairs came into sight, a wincing *oh crap* moment crossing my face, shielded from the sheriff fortunately since he walked behind me.

Didn't save me from the truth, however.

Nope, there was no disguising the small patch of empty ground marked where a gnome should have stood.

"You do recall someone broke in here at 2AM and threw a rock through my window," I countered before the sheriff could *ah-ha!* and accuse me of killing my neighbor, doing my best to minimize the importance of what was clearly the murder weapon with zero success, I might add.

"Likely story," he said, confirming my suspicion he couldn't care less about the rock, the window, the vandalism or anything else I might bring up. "You could have caught Kendall in here and bashed his head in. Or," now he appeared excited by possibilities, those narrowed eyes widening as he told himself stories that simply had no merit, "you killed him and dragged him to the beach then threw the rock through your own window to make it seem like he'd been here."

This was becoming truly preposterous. Surely even he could see the holes in such a suggestion? "Why," I said, cutting off his wander into fantasy with cold confidence and a growing irritation he even suspected me at all when it was obvious, I was a victim in all this, too, thank you. Alive, yes, but a victim regardless. Finally went on when he registered the one word with a pause of his own. "I repeat, *why*? Why would I draw any kind of attention to myself? Why implicate involvement in any way? Surely throwing a rock through my own window only makes me look guilty, all the more reason to attack the man." Wait, I didn't mean to imply I had. Whoops, backtrack in progress. "I wouldn't be stupid enough to bring this to your attention if I'd killed him." There, that was better.

Nope, not better. Perkins paused, face falling a little from the triumphant expression he'd been sporting to doubt and then resentment and an utterly physical refusal to listen to another word I said. "I'll figure it out," he said. "But it's clear you had more to do with this than you're saying, Ms. Pringle, and I'm going to find out what." He leaned in a little, animosity visible in his face. "We don't take kindly to strangers bringing their troubles to our town."

Um, hello? They had more than enough of their own disastrous messes, thank you. The fact I was caught up in it should have had this conversation flipped the other way around.

Maybe if he hadn't already written me off as a troublemaking tourist who riled up the locals, I might have stood a chance getting through to him. Not the case, was it? I could see it in his eyes, in the set of his shoulders. I wasn't endearing myself to the sheriff. When his own phone rang and, after a brief conversation that ended with him red-faced and furious, he spun on me like I'd insulted his beloved mother.

"Nice try on the FBI involvement," he said. "I won't hand over this case to someone you know. You can tell your agent husband to stay out of my business."

Trent. If I was going to murder anyone, it would be him. No regrets.

"Ex-husband," I said through clenched teeth, realizing what this was really about. Pride, really? A pointless competition over branches of law enforcement fed by too much testosterone? I should have kept my mouth shut, trusted myself, told Calliope nothing. All it got me was more trouble. And a meddling ex who didn't have the sense to let me handle things when we weren't even married anymore and he was no longer in any way, shape or form responsible for me or what I did.

Didn't do.

"Whatever." Sheriff Perkins's off-hand and casual derision elevated the issue far more than he knew. I *hated* that word. He had no idea how much. So dismissive, the ultimate insult. It was Trent's favorite preamble to the silent treatment, his brush-off of *done talking now* that triggered me like nothing else. Another tidbit to add to the list of things I had to handle before I could move on, I guess. Meanwhile, with no idea how close he'd come to being shot with his own gun, Sheriff Perkins handed off the gnome to his deputy who carried it through my side garden gate while I glared at the invasion of privacy. "Tell me again, Ms. Pringle, what happened last night."

"She killed him!" And just when I needed her most (yeah, right), Annie appeared over my fence to tighten the noose around my neck, and I finally had the answer to the question which neighbor was going to give me the most reason to tear my hair out. Because despite the fact he was dead and I was a suspect, the live one could still talk, right? Kind of wouldn't stop talking, actually, and really needed her to. "I saw her! I saw her kill him!" She hesitated then, confusion washing over her face. "No, I saw him kill her."

Okay, maybe she was more help than harm after all. Perkins had to see how befuddled and unbalanced she seemed. Taking her word for anything had to cross into the realm of the ludicrous.

I spun on the old woman, her pale eyes huge as she scowled at me, shaking one finger at me before catching herself as she started to topple.

"Annie, you didn't see me hurt anyone," I said. "And no one hurt me. Tell the truth, please."

My challenge had the opposite effect I'd hoped for, my choice to treat her like a misbehaving child backfiring. Vicious cunning woke in her eyes, lips thinning to a line as the sweet(ish) old lady transformed from a befuddled dear into the passionate head of a witch hunt. "I saw you, Mary," she hissed. "Saw it *all.*" Gestured imperiously at the sheriff, her motion almost knocking her free of the fence, her grasp to right herself completely erasing any credibility from her following demand. "Arrest her, officer. She's a murderer."

"My name isn't Mary," I said, turning to the sheriff then, lowering my voice though I knew she'd hear me anyway. "This woman has obvious mental health issues. You can't believe anything she says."

Perkins ignored me, nodding to Annie. "What did you see, Mrs. Layton?"

Was he kidding me right now? There was no way her testimony would stand up in court. How much more conspicuous could it be she suffered from some kind of dementia and yet, here he was, asking her for her testimony?

The moment I was free to go, I was leaving

this insane place in my dust and not looking back.

"They fought all the time," Annie said, wriggling her fingers on the lip of the fence, hopping up and down just a bit in her excitement. "I saw her, saw her out here last night."

Wait, I *had* seen Annie. "You were watching through the window," I said. "When I found the rock. Did you see who threw it, Annie?" Wait, was I asking her for help now when I just argued internally against her ability to remember clearly? Any port in a storm, except this one was filled with jagged rocks and death.

"You were dragging him," she said then, gaze flickering to the gate. "I saw you, you dragged him out into the sand and to the water, right through there." Her trembling hand gestured before returning to cling to the pickets. The sudden flicker of cruelty that passed across her face had me wondering which of the personas she displayed was the real Annie and which were figments of her imagination as she spiraled down into whatever diagnosis she'd been given. For Henry's sake, I hoped she'd been kind. Then again, her moments of niceness might have been a relief if she'd been cruel, while her newfound awful a terrible burden to bear.

I tapped my foot on the ground, crossing my arms over my chest, the unfairness of this entire ridiculous mess pushing me to the edge of petulance with this woman. Were she and her condition wearing off on me? "You watched me pull the lawn lounger to the beach." No amount of correcting her was going to change her mind and I knew it. Either she didn't want to because she was a heartless creature inside the frail form of a seemingly harmless and helpless old lady, or she honestly believed what she witnessed was true. In either case, I wasn't getting anywhere going about things this way. I made another effort, instead, to at least convince Perkins of my recollection of events, much more trustworthy than hers.

I pointed to the tracks the lounger made in the dirt near the exit, to the gate itself and the beach beyond. "Her timeline is totally off."

One of the deputies appeared at the back gate precisely as I indicated it, the other returning through my side one empty-handed. "Sheriff, Lou wants to talk to you."

Perkins jabbed his own finger at me then at the ground, his little *sit, stay, good dog* routine only increasing my blood pressure. I let him go without comment, spinning to glare at Annie, to find Henry there, whispering at her frantically.

"Henry, you have to talk to the sheriff," I said.

He glanced at me, guilty expression tight and anxious. "Just leave us out of it," he said. She batted at him when he pulled on her but finally relented, the two disappearing again while I fumed over their retreat.

If I ended up in jail for the night thanks to that old bird…

Maybe Trent wasn't the only person on my hit list.

CHAPTER ELEVEN

I should have anticipated Mitch's arrival, though when he hurried through the kitchen door to the garden I felt, as I had with the sheriff and deputies, an unhappy twinge that so many seemed to take my cottage rental as a thoroughfare. Mind you, this was Mitch's house, so he had a good reason to be here, though his concern for me rather than his property endeared him after the fact.

"Persephone," he almost tripped on his way down, wringing his hands, anxious expression and trembling voice all for me, "I'm so sorry you're having such a horrible experience." He shook his head, glancing at the gate to the beach. "How simply awful for you. This is just a disaster."

Tell me about it. "I'm sorry too, Mitch," I

said, "but the moment the sheriff clears me," he'd better, and fast, "I'm leaving."

The cottage owner nodded heavily, big hands clasping together in front of him as if in an attempt to stop their shaking. "Of course," he said. "I've already refunded your full deposit." He looked up again as a deputy appeared, lugging something heavy.

They couldn't be serious. With a fury that shocked me, I stormed to the gate and planted myself in the way, the young man's eyebrows shooting up, the body bag he held impacting him as whoever was on the far end was forced to a halt.

"No." My jaw ached from gritting my teeth. "Just. No."

The deputy actually gulped, bobbed a nod and jerked his head to the other one at the far end of the body. They retreated, though Lou Savoy and Sheriff Perkins apparently didn't get the memo, the two of them wandering through the gate while the deputies took the long way around.

"I'll do the autopsy right away," Lou said to Perkins before nodding to me. "Ms. Pringle, a delight to meet you, though I wish under different circumstances." He mopped at his face with that same damp handkerchief. "I'll have Linda stop by to see Candace, poor kid."

"Thanks, Lou." Perkins slapped the round man on the shoulder before turning to Mitch who shared a short greeting with the departing coroner. "Mitch."

"Tommy, this is crazy." My host gestured toward me. "You know my guest had nothing to do with Kendall's murder. There are more than enough locals who wanted him dead." Hadn't I said that very thing myself?

Perkins hadn't softened his stance any. "I'm the law around here, Mitch, not you." He glanced sideways at me before tipping his hat to my host. "I'll be in touch." He sauntered out, again through my side gate, while I bit my tongue until he was gone.

"Does no one respect privacy around here?" I suppose it made sense to use the garden gate, but this wasn't a public road.

Mitch shrugged, apology written all over him. "Everyone knows everyone," he said. "And where keys are kept. It's a small community, Persephone. Even during tourist season, people hate to lock their doors. We're pretty close-knit and though Kendall was a general pain to everyone, he was one of us." He stuck both hands in the pockets of his shorts before sighing. "Nothing like this ever happens. I'm so sorry it's happening to you."

"What about Candace's mother?" She'd

died just last year.

Mitch flinched at that, gaze going to the fence between his property and the Doiron's. "A tragic accident," he said. "Mary was on a ladder, and it slipped. She fell, died instantly. Terrible." He forced a small smile. "I'm having the boys come in to replace the window," he said. "Maybe you'd like to get out of the house, go for a walk in town? Get your mind off things?"

That was the last thing I wanted, especially knowing in small places like this word traveled fast and the fact I was prime suspect in a local's murder wasn't going to endear me to the populace. Still, it was clear I wasn't going to have any privacy here with workmen tromping around. And driving home wasn't an option, as much as I'd have liked to thumb my nose at the sheriff and his small-minded need to protect his territory.

Maybe Mitch was right and a stroll in the sunshine that didn't involve finding a corpse might cheer me up a little. A coffee, even. Surely, this town had coffee?

I grabbed my purse and slung it across my body, heading down the lane with sunglasses hiding my eyes, hands in my pockets, knowing this was a terrible idea but hopefully things couldn't get any worse. Actually found, as my sandals kicked stray stones and the asphalt turned to cobbles as I turned at the corner and was suddenly on the main street that the walk was doing me good. While I garnered a few stares and whispers, no one bothered me, allowing me to examine the picturesque little shops from outside, to pause at a small cart for a hot cup of java from an adorable elderly woman who didn't seem to know or care who I was, and finally to pause by what looked like an empty lot converted into a small farmer's market.

I hadn't expected to run into Candace, the young woman standing behind one of the booths with an older lady who hugged her suddenly. Part of me wanted to duck for cover, but as I contemplated abandoning my walk and my coffee and making a run for it, Candace spotted me. Waved for me to join them, her expression softly sad but without the accusatory anger I'd been prepared for.

I joined her at the WHOLESOME FARM stand, the logo on her t-shirt I'd noticed the day before of a smiling pig matching the one over the counter. She worked there, apparently, the woman next to her offering her hand over a tray of strawberries that smelled so good I was drooling.

"Theresa Ellis," she said, dark tan and sun-bleached hair signs of long days in the elements, as were the lines around her green eyes. "You must be Ms. Pringle. Staying at Mitch and Sherry's place, right?" She grimaced then. "Sorry, Sunshine Cottage."

Mitch was married? I hadn't heard anything about a wife, now embarrassed by my mental leap he might misconstrue my friendliness. Focused on the trembling girl instead of my questions. "Candace, I'm so sorry," I said after nodding to Theresa.

She was back to hugging herself, though she didn't look like she was in shock any longer, rather deep in acceptance, a quick transition for someone who'd experienced so much loss so quickly. "I know you weren't responsible," she said. "And you're right. Everyone hated Dad. So, we may never know who killed him." She said it so matter-of-factly even Theresa seemed shocked, one hand on the girl's shoulder as she exchanged a worried look with me.

"If there's anything I can do." I fumbled out one of my cards, handed it to her. "I already offered, and that offer is even more important now."

Candace nodded, sniffled, shrugged. "Thanks," she said. Turned to Theresa. "Sorry about my shift." Then left, quietly and without fuss while I second-guessed my diagnosis and wondered if she was now in a daze instead of an advanced stage of grief.

"That poor dear," Theresa said, drawing my attention back. "She's been through so much this year. Just awful. She and Mary were so close." She leaned in toward me, eyes a little wide. "Is it true someone hit him and left him to drown?"

That was a lot of detail for someone not in the sheriff's department to have on hand, though it was possible Candace told her.

When I didn't answer right away, Theresa retreated, though I noted a pair of older ladies lingered and figured not only had the rumor mill been working overtime, but gossip was a mainstay of this place, like most small towns.

"I'm sure the sheriff will find out what happened," I said, knowing my tone was weak and lacked conviction.

Theresa seemed to agree with my attitude if not my words, snorting. "Perkins is an ass and useless," she said. "If I were you, I'd make a run for it before he figures out how to blame a stranger."

I was not about to tell her he already had. "I didn't realize my host was married," I said. "Are they from Zephyr?"

Theresa's guilty look returned. "My bad," she said. "Sherry and their son, Isaac, left about six months ago. I keep forgetting, such a shame."

Maybe the reason Mitch was so overeager to please? Didn't matter at the moment, but knowing we had that in common did increase my feeling of kinship toward the man. "Then you must know Annie and Henry Layton?" Maybe Theresa could confirm what I already suspected, that the old lady was off her rocker.

"Of course," she smiled. "Both born and raised right here in Zephyr." The two ladies lingering drew a little closer while I did my best to phrase my next question carefully.

"I noticed Annie seems to struggle with names and times," I said. "Is that common?"

Before Theresa could answer, one of our eavesdroppers tittered. "Annie Layton should be in a home," she said while her friend tried to shush her, blushing and tugging on her to go. "She's more than poor Henry can handle any longer. I swear, she'll be the death of him and then what will happen to her?"

The two ladies left then, arguing quietly as they walked off, Theresa's expression tight with resignation and amusement.

"Annie's been declining a few years now," she said. "It's an old town." She shrugged, looked around and I realized she was right. Aside from Candace and the two deputies, most of the people I'd met or seen were older, at least my age. "Our town won't last much longer, I reckon, not unless we do something about it."

The plight of many small towns, sadly, as the young people moved away, looking for opportunities. "I take it you have an idea?" Of course, she did.

Theresa sighed over her vegetables and fruit, arms crossing, sadness on her lined face. "The only thing that seems to work is tourism," she said. "There was supposed to be a new hotel resort built here last year, but it fell through. Most folks lost a lot of money because of it." Wait, was that what the sheriff meant when he spoke to Mitch yesterday, how the townsfolk had lost out last year? "Everyone invested so we could make it a community project, so everyone would benefit. But when the deal fell through…" Theresa offered me a box of strawberries which I accepted, slipping them into a mesh bag she supplied. "Kind of knocked the wind out of everyone's sails, you know what I mean?"

I bet. That kind of disappointment could also lead to other problems. "Why did the deal fall through?"

Theresa's lips thinned to a tight line. "One of the homeowners wouldn't agree to it," she said. "We needed the property."

Oh boy. "Let me guess," I said. "Kendall Doiron."

"And his wife, Mary," Theresa agreed. Leaned in again, whispering this time. "You want to know who killed him? Whoever lost the most money last year, that's who."

"That being?" I handed over a pair of dollars in payment while she winked.

"Sheriff Perkins," she said.

CHAPTER TWELVE

Well now, wasn't *that* interesting to hear? "Is there any chance the hotel might go ahead now if there's no opposition?" Certainly sounded sketchy on the sheriff's part. Was Perkins pushing me to the top of the suspect list to keep himself from that position? I'd already promised myself I'd stop jumping to conclusions, but it had a ring of truth to it that I couldn't drop. Money was an excellent motivator for murder, either gaining a lot or otherwise. Definitely wouldn't be the first time someone's death was motivated by the loss of it.

Theresa brightened just a little before a guilty look crept in and took over, frown deepening, eyes tight. "I shouldn't hope so on Kendall's account," she said. "That's horrible, isn't it?"

"*He* was horrible," I said, so offhand she laughed, laughed with her at the cynical statement that had more truth than not, and dead guy notwithstanding, truth was funny.

"He was at that," she agreed. "If we are going to move ahead with the resort, though, I don't doubt a lot of folks will struggle to come up with the capital." She tossed her hands. "Too little, too late. You know what, though." Theresa snapped her fingers. "If anyone could fill you in, it would be Ellen at town hall." She winked. "Ellen Morrison. She's the mayor's clerk and has all the gossip. Tell her I sent you to be nosy."

I thanked her for the information and left, munching fresh strawberries from the bag while juggling my coffee, finally dumping it in a trash bin across the street from the sheriff's office. It made perfect sense to me that he'd try to saddle me with the murder if he was involved. I debated a visit to see Theresa's friend, Ellen and decided against it shortly after abandoning my prickly plan to confront the sheriff with what I now knew. Neither would get me anywhere. If Perkins was behind Kendall's murder, it wasn't like he'd tell me and since he was the law around here, the only way I'd get justice is to call outside his jurisdiction which meant calling Trent which was not going to happen. And so, what if the hotel deal was back up and running? While it was pretty quick considering Kendall was barely cold, it meant nothing to me aside from possible motivation for Perkins to kill Kendall and that just took me back in the same circle I'd just walked because apparently, I had a thing for redundant meandering and wasted mental energy on things I couldn't change.

Tired, hot and over this entire idea, all I wanted suddenly was to go back to my cottage, have a shower and a nap and a gin and maybe forget for a bit that someone died on the beach.

Except, the workmen were still there when I arrived so my hope for a quiet late morning was dashed as they fiddled with the new window. Fine. If I was going to be forced by circumstance into figuring out how to remove myself from the list of suspects, I'd stop fighting fate and get it over with. Which meant climbing into my SUV for a short drive, too warm and weary to walk to the other end of town where my phone's map service said I'd find my destination.

It was hot and sticky inside, so I fired up the engine and let it run a moment, retreating inside while the air conditioning did its job, returning after changing into a fresh set of clothes, adding a touch of mascara and lip gloss, dumping my purse in favor of just my wallet and phone, feeling a bit more refreshed after splashing my face and neck with water and having a long drink of the same.

The last thing I expected when I opened the door to my now cool interior was for the streak of fluffy white to appear out of nowhere and leap up onto the driver's seat, the gorgeous but uninvited guest blinking those green eyes at me before Belladonna dodged my attempt to grab her and hopped over the console into the back.

"Excuse me, miss," I said.

She ignored me, settling down on all four feet, hunching over them. But when I sighed and opened the back door to try to scoot her out, she easily dodged me, doing another acrobatic hop to the passenger's side.

Seriously, outdone by a cat? I wasn't having the best day, was I?

I finally shrugged and climbed in, Belladonna curling up on the seat next to me, blinking a few times before settling down for the ride. She seemed comfortable enough when I cranked the air conditioning even further and let the sultry tones of the British hottie guide me across town.

My hitchhiker's presence meant I left the SUV running outside Peaceful Rest Funeral

Home so the silly cat wouldn't cook herself, shaking my head and snorting as I locked her inside in the comfort of blowing air while I made my way inside the mortuary.

Lou himself stood at the front counter, soft strains of soothing music the perfect undertone to the place, thick, green carpeting and dark-paneled walls a dim and suitably solemn environment. As for the mortician himself, he beamed a happy smile at my arrival, waving off the woman he'd been speaking to as she hurried out the front door with a little nod for me.

"Linda is off to see Candace," he said. "What can I do for you, Ms. Pringle?"

"Persephone, please," I said. Hesitated. "Mr. Savoy—"

"Just Lou," he said, eyes sparkling with good humor. "You're wondering what I found?"

"I know you can't talk to me," I said. "I don't really know why I'm here except the sheriff seems to think I'm involved, and I need answers." Wow, did I really sound that pathetically desperate? Was I actually worried Perkins might successfully pin this on me? Or was I just at a limit of last nerves and disappointment and second-guessing that had me feeling vulnerable?

The last, without a doubt. Fortunately for me, I came to the right place.

Lou gently guided me to a set of antique chairs next to the double doors leading into the parlor. Empty, thankfully, though no doubt this was where Kendall Doiron's service would be held. I wondered if anyone would show up, felt instantly guilty at the thought and sagged while the lovely man with the huge heart and visible compassion patted my hand.

"I can tell you Kendall died from a blow to the head," he said. "And that the garden gnome was the murder weapon. It's possible he slipped and fell and hit his head, however. Though if it was an accident, how he ended up in the water—and the gnome in the sand—is up for debate."

"Do you have a time of death?" It felt awkward to ask that, like I was some kind of sleuth in a TV murder mystery who really needed to back off and keep her head down and on her shoulders before the real killer came for her for being a nosy Nelly.

Whew. Time to slow down my brain before I had a stroke.

"Likely around the same time as the vandalism at the cottage," Lou said then. "It's hard when water is involved, temperature adjustments and whatnot, but my best estimation is about 2AM."

At least he hadn't been dead out there on the beach waiting for someone to find him while I worried about a rock through my window. Which had me thinking all over again he'd done the deed, been returning home, and, what? Encountered a stray garden gnome in the wild?

I had a brief thought about Annie, her attachment to the thing. Discarded that idea since Kendall had at least a foot of height and a lot of weight on the slight old lady. How would she even have reached him to hit him? And what possible motivation would she have had for hurting him? No telling, I suppose, in her mental condition. Though, what if Lou was right and she accidentally left it lying around on the beach, he tripped and…

Then how did he end up in the water?

So many questions and answers I really shouldn't have been seeking because I wasn't a cop, for goodness' sake. I was a therapist. I had to get my priorities straight.

"Thank you for being honest with me," I said. "Lou, I understand there were a lot of people angry with Kendall because of the hotel deal falling through." So much for priorities and dropping it and all that. I had an issue with letting things go that was now on my list of what was wrong with me I needed to fix before it got me in more trouble.

Lou sat back, nodding, pudgy hands folding over his round belly, genuine regret on his face. "Linda and I lost a tidy sum," he said, "but many people ended up losing their life savings. It was a horrible time, just horrible." He seemed to connect my question with the present, though not with any sort of surprise. "You've put together the same scenario I have, then," he said. "Clever of you, Persephone. I would think it's obvious, even to an outsider, that whoever wanted Kendall dead likely held a grudge from that time that finally came to a head." He winced then chuckled. "Forgive the terrible reference."

I grinned back, unable to stop myself. His good humor had an infectious quality that I appreciated. "I was told the person who lost the most might be the one investigating this very crime."

Lou's eyebrows shot up, though he did give it a deep think before rubbing at his chin with one thumb, eyes narrowing at last. "I hate to admit it," he said, "or think badly of my neighbors. I suppose Tommy Perkins had as much motive as any of us." He nodded to me. "Including me." He settled both hands on his thighs as he pushed himself to his feet before offering me assistance to stand myself. I took it, not because I needed it, but because he was a gentleman. "One thing is certain in my mind, Persephone. You didn't kill Kendall Doiron."

"You have evidence?" I wished.

"I know people." He shrugged at that. "Honestly, you know who I'm worried most about?" Lou hesitated before he met my eyes again with his own full of anxiety, voice dropping when he spoke next. "Candace."

He said what now? "You think she could have killed her own father?" My mind flashed to her state, her quick recovery from grief, her dazed and abrupt manner. Could it have been, instead of sorrow, a show of guilt she struggled with?

Lou seemed instantly regretful, shaking his head. "No, of course not," he said. Then paused. "Except, well. There was… some possibility. About her mother's passing." He finally sagged as though deciding to just say it instead of beating bushes. "That it might not have been an accident."

"Candace killed her mother?" Wow, was the young woman some kind of parental serial killer?

But Lou's sadness said otherwise. "Not Candace." Stopped.

Oh. Oh, dear.

CHAPTER THIRTEEN

I said my goodbyes and thank yous, the drive back to the cottage wrapped up in a lot of questions.

"There was no solid evidence someone tampered with the ladder," Lou had hurriedly assured me. "It was just something Candace said. At the funeral. She asked me if there was. If it was possible. I didn't know what to tell her, kept it to myself when she asked me to. But now, in light of her father's death…"

If Candace lived the last year thinking her father killed her mother, it was very possible he finally pushed her too far and she did away with him to avenge the loss.

I had almost completely forgotten about Belladonna, parking the car and turning off the engine, opening the door with my mind whirling, only to have her leap over me and out the door, bounding away without a backward look.

"You're welcome for the ride, your highness," I called after her. Didn't expect an answer and didn't get one. Instead, I headed inside, the work truck gone from the street and, to my relief, not a workman in sight.

In fact, not only was the window replaced, but someone had delivered fresh groceries. Of course, that someone had to have been Mitch, the note inside the bag along with a second bottle of gin—my brand, even, though the fact he knew that was a bit creepy—and an assortment of goodies that had me drooling and realizing it was after lunch and I was living on the faint remains of berries and a half bowl of cereal.

A small apology, his note read. *I'll speak to the sheriff personally. I hope you enjoy the rest of your stay, on me.*

I hoped so, too, though the odds were not in my favor.

Then again, I had gin, food and sunshine. Privacy at last. And nothing to do but relax and wait for the sheriff to finally come to his senses before I brought in a lawyer. By the time I made a lovely curried chicken and rice for lunch and devoured it over a drink, I was feeling much better. Of course, I had nothing to worry about. No court would even consider the case against me as anything but a joke. All that remained was to be patient and carry on with my retreat as best I could until I was able to get out of Zephyr.

I hesitated over using the lawn lounger now that I knew how familiar everyone was with each other's properties, but it was so beautiful out, I couldn't resist. Of course, the fact someone died on the beach should also have been a deterrent, but a second gin in hand and the reminder that Kendall Doiron had already ruined the bulk of my time here had me determined to not let him complete the job.

The sound of children laughing further down the shore toward town brought a smile to my face, the stretch I was on deserted for the time being. I highly doubted Candace would make a sunbathing appearance which left Annie and Henry on the right. Somehow, they didn't seem the tanning kind. So, as long as no one took a stroll this way, I'd have the beach to myself.

Perfecto.

Sipping and listening to music had a cathartic effect to the point I found myself drifting off under the heat of the sun, forcing myself to flip over after a half hour so I didn't burn, drowsing in the warmth and finally relaxed.

"Mary?" That querulous voice woke me with a snort. I sat up abruptly, spotting Annie at the edge of the water, the tide returning though a few pools remained. She didn't address me, however, focusing instead on the distant horizon. The old lady had wandered into the ocean, hem of her dress wet, where she'd paused, hands wringing in front of her as if seeing someone out there in the waves no one else could. "Mary, are you there?"

I was up and after her with my heart in my throat, not bothering to throw on my cover up because if anyone had trouble seeing a fifty-year-old woman with a lot of tattoos and a few (ahem) extra pounds running around in a bikini, they could just keep it to themselves.

"Annie," I said, catching her arm gently so as not to startle her, smiling when she spun on me and laughed her cackle.

"Mary!" She hugged me tight, surprisingly strong for someone who looked so frail. "You shouldn't let Candace swim alone so young, Mary," she said, tsking her chastisement while I led her back to shore. "She's gone out too far on her own."

"She's all right," I said. "She's safe, Annie." Definitely dementia, possibly Alzheimer's with other complications layered into the mix. Now that she wasn't accusing me of murder, I knew better than to challenge her or force her to come back and face the present. Correcting her would only upset her and accomplish nothing. "Can I get you some tea?"

She patted my guiding hand, smiling up at me with a sweetness I hadn't seen on her face before. Was this the woman she used to be? "You're so kind to me, Mary," she said. "Thank you, dear. Henry and I are so grateful."

Clearly, the two had been friends, or at least happy neighbors. "Annie, do you remember the day I fell?" I asked her before I could stop myself, instantly regretting it when she stopped, eyes filling with tears, lower lip trembling."

"He pushed you," she whispered, grasping at my hands in scrabbling desperation. "But you're here, you're okay." Annie's disorientation was visibly devolving, a distant and troubled look crossing her face as she struggled with her disease and the memories she couldn't trust anymore. "Where are we?" She looked up at me, alarm now settling in, fear even, as her mind failed her completely and wiped her slate clean for a moment. "Who are you?" How often did she reset like this? I felt a surge of compassion for Henry while I let her go, knowing again if I fought her in this state, it would end badly.

She stepped clear of me, trying to walk backward but tripping over her own feet, landing hard in the sand. Burst into tears like a hurt toddler as I spotted Henry hobbling toward us from their garden gate, calling her name, his range of motion obviously compromised.

I helped her up as he made it to his wife, breathing heavily, huffing her name. He tugged her toward him while she fought him off, her tears dried up.

"Leave me be," she snarled at him. Looked up at me. "I'm glad he pushed you," she said, then giggled wickedly.

Henry's obvious horror had him spluttering, trying to cover what she'd just said even as he fought to catch his breath, face flushed with more than just exertion. "She doesn't know what she's saying half the time."

I nodded. "I know the signs of dementia, Henry." He seemed on the verge of tears himself. "Did she tell you that Kendall pushed Mary?"

He hesitated, jaw jumping, hands tightening on his wife who now hummed and picked at a band-aid on the back of her hand. "I don't want to get involved," he said.

"If Annie saw Kendall murder Mary, you need to tell someone." Henry was already moving, dragging Annie away, while I followed at a slower pace, knowing there was nothing I could do, that the old man was only doing what he thought best, protecting his sick wife.

And he was right. Getting involved meant putting Annie and her illness under a microscope. And she clearly had time and memory issues, so did she even see what she thought she did? More likely he worried if anyone knew how sick she was he might be forced to put her in care.

Regardless of his motives, Henry managed to maneuver Annie through their garden gate and close it firmly behind him while I stood there on the beach and wondered why I cared.

Except all I could think about was Calliope. And Candace. All while comparing my daughter to the poor young woman next door who very possibly knew her father killed her mother and then murdered him when she couldn't live with it anymore.

None of my business but a heartbreaking possibility I just couldn't let go of.

The question was, would Candace tell me the truth?

CHAPTER FOURTEEN

Despite the fact her scooter was missing, I chose to knock anyway, though it was obvious Candace wasn't home. Second-guessing the entire thing was easy enough to do as I retreated back to the cottage. I suppose I shouldn't have been surprised when Mitch pulled into the driveway behind my SUV as I paused by the side door, though my reaction to his kind concern was simply to wish he'd leave me alone.

Not to be ungrateful, but my attempted retreat was turning into a circus.

He waved as he walked the short distance up the drive, my own hand rising in response before I could stop it while I'm positive the tight smile I managed wouldn't have passed much muster under normal circumstances.

Mitch paused beside me, making no attempt to enter, at least, his anxiety still visible as if he'd been the one who'd been accused of murder.

"I just wanted to be sure the workmen did the job okay," he said. "And to check in on you. Are you doing all right?"

Any snarky reaction I might have fired off was smothered by my reminder to myself this was far from the poor man's fault, and he didn't deserve such from tired and increasingly cranky me.

"I'm fine, Mitch, thank you. For the groceries and the gin. And yes, the window is all fixed." Really, that was the best I could manage. Wouldn't he just leave now before I had to ask him to?

"I really am terribly sorry about all this." He'd apologized sufficiently, no more required, but he didn't seem to think so.

"It's pretty obvious to me you've had difficulties with Kendall Doiron in the past," I said. Kind of an accusation, even if I hadn't meant it to come out that way. Well, maybe I had, but not in as blunt a manner. I really was tired.

Mitch's face fell, lengthening out into regret with more apologies pending, I was sure. "The sheriff assured me he'd no longer be a problem," he said. Swallowed hard. "He's just insufferable." Paused. "Was, I mean."

No kidding. "I understand he lost his wife last year," I said.

My host's expression tightened as he glanced toward the Doiron house. "A tragedy," he said. "A terrible accident, from what I heard."

"Someone mentioned it may not have been an accident." If he was going to linger, the least I could do was pull out some gossip.

But Mitch's wide eyes and shock felt so authentic he clearly hadn't heard that rumor himself. "How horrible," he said. Before whispering, "Do they think Kendall did it?"

Apparently jumping to that conclusion was the natural assumption.

"I'm hoping the sheriff will relent by the morning," I said, reaching for the door handle and opening it, stepping half inside, hoping he'd take it as a dismissal. When he didn't move, just bobbed a nod, I plastered on that smile again. "I'm going to try to take a nap. Thanks for checking in." And firmly closed the door behind me without looking back.

The sound of Mitch's car firing up and driving off had me breathing a sigh of relief and promising myself the next time I decided to do something like this I'd make sure to do a lot more research.

I poured a glass of gin, realizing if I was going to keep up this pace, I'd be cracking the one Mitch bought me before nightfall, shrugged and headed outside. Rather than the garden and the prying eyes of Annie and her husband, however, I chose the side porch around the corner and the swing I had as yet to try. Except it was already occupied, the fluffy white creature grooming her lovely tail pausing to examine my arrival with those bright, green eyes. She didn't seem to mind me settling next to her, polite enough to take up one side of the swing instead of the whole thing. When I didn't make any further moves, she went back to her grooming, the hum of the returning scooter catching my attention.

Thanks to the elevation of the porch and swing I could easily see over the fence and waved at Candace as she returned. She hesitated a moment before coming to join me, circling to the side gate at the top of my driveway and through, climbing two of the three steps with her helmet clutched in both hands.

When she caught sight of Belladonna next to me, however, Candace's reticence vanished in a soft sound of happiness when she looked back and forth between us.

"She doesn't like anyone," she said. Shook

her head. "Doesn't like *me*. Hated Dad. Bella was my mother's cat. She got her as a kitten only six months before she died." Candace choked up a little, took a moment to clear her throat, though she did take that last step and joined me, leaning against the railing, setting her helmet aside and redoing her ponytail to tame the escaped flyaways that clung to her face. "I think she likes you."

I slowly reached out to the cat, stroked her fur. Belladonna's purr fired up instantly, her cheek pressing into my fingers when I scratched. "She's beautiful," I said.

Candace sighed, so soft and sad I looked up again to find her crying, though silently, wiping at tears and then rubbing her hands against her jean shorts to dry them away.

"Candace," I said, "can I offer you a drink?" I had enough gin in my own bottle for that.

She seemed surprised by the offer, shy smile emerging through her tears. "Thank you," she said. "I'd like that."

Two minutes later she sat next to me, the pair of us swinging, Belladonna napping against my hip, sipping gin and cranberry while the young woman finally seemed to relax.

"You don't have to be kind," she said. "I know what my father was like. And honestly, Mom wasn't much better. Everyone tries to be nice about it, to say nice things. But they weren't friendly people, so it feels fake, you know?"

I nodded. "Nothing annoys me more than hypocrisy after the fact."

"Exactly." She took another drink. "This is delicious. I've never had gin before."

The thought struck me I was feeding alcohol to a minor, but she laughed and shook her head at my moment of whoops. "Just turned twenty-one. Promise. I just… I've never had many friends. Most of the kids I went to high school with live in other towns or left for college or the city before now." I'd noticed that, been informed of that very fact by Theresa Ellis.

"Your parents opposed the hotel," I said, being gentle but letting her know I wasn't ignorant of local politics. "That couldn't have been easy, either."

Candace shrugged, staring down into the drink, lips twisting with enough bitterness I knew she held onto a lot of anger toward her parents, and not just thanks to the hotel issue. "It was impossible to make them happy," she blurted then. Took a long drink. Coughed, cleared her throat, cheeks red with emotion. "They were my parents and I loved them, but I didn't like either of them very much."

"Did you think about leaving?" That would have been the easiest route.

Candace's snort of derision answered that question. "I tried to go," she said. "Got accepted into college. But they refused to pay for it, said I was old enough to take care of my own school. The problem is, I couldn't get a loan because they made too much money. So, I was stuck." There was the resentment again, and for good reason. What parents didn't want to help their children get ahead in life? I hadn't liked Kendall Doiron from the moment he almost hit me, but my estimation of both he and his wife had plummeted despite their early passings.

I hated to think it because I was better than that, but maybe the young woman was better off without such a terrible burden in her life.

"I bet you were wondering why I wasn't broken up over Dad's death." Candace finished her drink, setting it in her lap, turning it around and around, her thumb tracing a pattern through the condensation. "I just can't fake it. Yes, I'm sad he's gone, that she's gone. But I can't bring myself to grieve over them like I should."

"Everyone has their own ways of dealing with death," I said, softly touching her on the wrist before pulling back again. "No judging,

Candace. You get to feel exactly how you need to feel. There could come a time when you do grieve them like you think you should. But there's absolutely nothing wrong with how you're feeling about them right now."

She blinked at me, tears clinging to her long lashes, though she smiled, a real smile that crinkled the corners of her eyes. "Thank you," she said. "I needed to hear that." Candace let out a long, slow breath, hands stilling at last, the feeling of relaxation that had started when she sat spinning down into a more settled sense of calm. "Can I tell you something and you promise not to tell anyone else?"

Since I'd been looking for an in, her sudden question had me almost breathless with hope I wouldn't have to bring it up after all, that she might open to me without me having to ask her outright about her father's death.

"That depends," I said, deciding to be completely honest. "If I'm listening as a friend and you tell me something that might mean you're in danger or someone else was hurt, I'd be obligated to tell the police. But if I'm your therapist, I'd be under confidentiality rules. I'd still do everything I could to make sure you were okay, but I couldn't do anything to put you in harm's way even if you revealed something to me that might, say, solve a crime."

She stared at me in silence a long moment, her smile gone, expression empty, before she nodded. "I'd like to hire you," she said.

"Done," I said. "What did you need to tell me?" Was it wrong I felt a thrill of excitement mixed with horrified certainty when she spoke next?

"I think my father murdered my mother," she said, confirming the first part of my guesswork. "And I have proof."

CHAPTER FIFTEEN

Wait, she made no mention of revenge, of killing her father in turn. Did that mean she was innocent? Believe me, I'd have been more than happy to scratch Candace off the suspect list. But, if she did have proof Kendall killed Mary, why had she held onto it for so long? And would she actually admit it to me if she had murdered her father to avenge her mother?

On the other hand, she'd just finished telling me she didn't like her parents much, so would her mother's murder motivate her to finish the job? Maybe if having her father out of the picture meant the kind of freedom she craved.

I was jumping ahead of myself at a rapid-fire pace while Candace collected her thoughts and then interrupted my mental gymnastics with her soft, sad words.

"I found his shoe print," she said. "In the dirt. Next to the ladder." The ice left in the bottom of her glass tinkled when her fingers trembled, lower lip following, though she carried on. "I was the one who found her. Thought at first it was an accident, like everyone else. Except Dad was in the house, why didn't he check on her? She must have made a noise as she fell. I was in the driveway and heard the crash." The young woman looked up at last, tears tricking down her cheeks, voice tight with emotion she'd clearly been hanging onto far too long. "He must have heard." She shook her head, more strands escaping her vain attempt to corral her thin, dark hair in the elastic. "I ran to check, found Mom dead. Her neck snapped when she hit the ground." Candace swiped at her nose with the shoulder of her t-shirt, snuffling. "At least, that's what Lou said."

"I'm so sorry," I said. "She didn't suffer?"

Candace shook her head again. "Lou said she died on impact. So, there's that." She shifted on the bench, rocking the swing a little, Belladonna looking up as if irritated by the disturbance. "I screamed for Dad, and he finally came out, took one look at Mom and went back inside. He didn't seem to care." She made a more aggressive attempt to scrub tears from her face with the hem of her shirt, pulling herself together, weeping over, jaw tight as anger returned. "He called the sheriff, but he didn't come out again. He left me alone with Mom."

If Kendall Doiron had been alive and next door I would have marched over there and kicked his behind personally. As it was, all I could do was reach out and squeeze Candace's hand. She hung onto me, fingers cold and clammy from the surface of the glass, trembling in mine.

"That's when I saw his shoe print," she said.

"Did you tell the sheriff?" I wasn't holding out hope Perkins paid attention regardless, but when Candace indicated to the negative, I had to cut him a break. On this, at least.

"I scuffed it out with my sneaker," she said. "For all I knew, Dad had been in the garden and the print was old." She didn't sound like she believed that. "Mom wasn't supposed to be up the ladder. She agreed to hire someone to clean the eavestroughs. She and Dad fought about it because she wanted him to do it and he refused. They fought all the time." Candace's grip on me tightened as her temper flared. "*All* the time. About stupid stuff no one should fight about." She only then seemed to realize she was using my hand as a stress ball and loosened her grip, though I gently squeezed back so she would know it was okay. "I can't prove he did it, but I'm sure he did. He never walked in the garden. That was Mom's domain. The only reason he would have had to stand by the ladder was to push her."

"You think they were arguing, and he knocked the ladder over in anger?" It did make sense. People were known to react in the heat of the moment and regret such actions later. A simple shove out of rage would have been enough. And her description of him hiding in the house certainly felt like a guilt reaction.

Candace sighed deeply, sipping a bit of melted ice from the bottom of her glass before staring out over the fence at her property. "I don't know," she said. "But I wouldn't have put it past him. I've lived with it for a year, Persephone. The idea that he killed my mother and just left her there." Ah. Here it was, then. Her own confession. Surely, she was about to tell all? Except her anger had faded back to sorrow and she seemed drained enough, replete, which suggested to me in my professional opinion, she was done with her story.

Someone who'd committed murder would carry more tension, more potential for reveal.

Candace had neither. Which meant I'd jumped to the wrong conclusion after all.

Trust me, I was very happy to know it. The poor girl had been through enough.

"I'm selling the house," she said then, calm returned. "I can't wait to get out of there."

"That was quick," I said, but with enough approval in my voice when she met my smile she smiled back. "Good for you, Candace."

"The hotel people were happy to finally get a yes," she said.

Wait, the deal was back on after all? "I bet," I said. "When did you find out?"

"That's where I was," she said. "They called me about an hour ago. I just signed the paperwork." Candace grinned, a rueful little expression. "Don't worry, they didn't take me for a ride. I know what the house is worth and held out for extra." Good for her. "I'm just happy it's over. I'll be here when they take the place down. Might even help."

That was enough firm decisiveness I didn't worry about her state of mind.

"Why didn't your parents sell, Candace? I hear the deal was a very good one, that the whole town was going to benefit. That many even invested." Seemed odd to me.

Until Candace barked a little laugh. "Precisely because it was good for Zephyr," she said. "My parents didn't get along with anyone here in case you missed it. And pissing people off seemed to amuse them."

Amazing she turned out as well as she did.

Candace turned to me then as the big, white cat stood and stretched, letting out a purring murmur before turning in place and settling again, this time with her chin on my thigh. Sorrow passed over the young woman's face, but she was smiling.

"I need to find a home for Belladonna," she said. "I don't want any reminders, especially not her. It's too hard. And she deserves a happy home." Candace looked up, met my eyes. "If you'd consider it, I'd let you take her."

That was the last offer I'd been expecting, knowing my eyes flew wide, eyebrows almost to my hairline, while my hand immediately fell to stroke the cat's fur.

Wait, was I actually considering it?

Candace wrinkled her nose, a happy smile now on her face, the last of her tears and anger gone, faint shrug shifting her shoulders. "Think about it," she said. Stood. "I have to go sort through what I need to pack and what I want to take. It won't be much."

I waved goodbye, sat there for a long time with the sleeping cat, trying to reconcile what Candace told me with what I knew. While a twinge of intuition whispered I was missing something.

Whether Belladonna sensed my unrest or was just done with her nap, she rose, stretched and hopped down, sashaying her way over the porch's edge and into the flower bed, disappearing into the foliage. While I stood and headed for the garden, the missing gnome. Took a closer look at the ground.

Noted the imprint of a shoe. Headed for the gate, the sand on the other side.

Same shoe.

Kendall's shoe?

Enough people had been through here and the side gate it was possibly the sheriff's or Lou's or even one of the deputies. Except it was smooth bottomed like Kendall wore. Was this proof he'd been in the garden?

Like the sheriff cared about proof.

For the briefest of moments, I considered calling Trent, imagine that. Squashed that particular bout of weakness with a firm and confident hand and, destination in mind and time on my hands an excuse to walk to town, I headed out to do my own research.

After all, if Sheriff Perkins was going to insist I stay until he said so, I'd just have to find a way to convince him to let me go.

Amazing how easy it was sometimes to

convince myself truly terrible ideas had perfectly logical merit. That's how I ended up with a smile fixed on my face for the woman behind the counter at town hall, asking a question I hoped she could answer.

"Ellen, right?" I poured on the charm and professional charisma as she immediately smiled back, the middle-aged woman (why did I still feel like I was twenty-five and not twice that?) in the twinset and pearls (please, please don't ever let me turn into a middle-aged woman for reals) and matching blue eyeshadow, nylons (gag) and comfortable shoes (dying). "Theresa told me to pop in if I had questions."

"Oh, how lovely," Ellen said. "What can I do for you, Mrs…?"

There it was again. "Persephone Pringle," I said. "I'm wondering if you have any information on the current state of the hotel development. If it's public record, that is."

Her smile flickered. "As a matter of fact, yes. Now that opposition is no longer an issue." She blushed, stammered a moment. "I didn't mean it that way. It's horrible Kendall passed. But obviously, someone alerted the chain because as of this afternoon the deal was back on." With Candace's signature, no doubt, as the clincher. Was that someone who contacted the resort developers perhaps the same soul who ensured things would move ahead with killer encouragement? Ellen paused, cocking her head to one side, appearing hesitant to go on before she spoke with curiosity of her own. "Planning on buying some property, Mrs. Pringle?"

I didn't bother correcting her. "You know what," I said, "I just might." When every single layer of this particular level of hell froze over.

Ellen glanced down at her desk, the top of the counter hiding what she was reading. "I'm so sorry," she said, "but I'll have to put that information together for you in the morning. It's 5PM." Her apologetic nose scrunch had me wondering if she really was sorry.

"No problem," I said, handing over my card. "Whenever you can." Left, fully expecting to never hear from her and thoroughly over this town. And my ridiculous efforts to, what, convince the hard-nosed and incompetent sheriff I didn't kill a total stranger? All while ready to put everything to do with Zephyr, Maine, in my rearview once and for all.

At least I had gin. I had a feeling I was going to need it.

CHAPTER SIXTEEN

I wasn't even upset when I arrived at the cottage to find Mitch's car in the driveway, nor to find the man himself bent over in the garden, replacing, of all things, the hideous garden gnome that killed Kendall Doiron with, you guessed it, a new one. An exact replica, as far as I could tell, minus the human element.

Lovely. And, I guess, rather fitting considering the rest of this odd and uncomfortable trip.

He looked up, a bit red in the face from failing to bend at the knees. "Sorry for the intrusion again," he said, nodding genially toward me as I took the steps to the kitchen door, bending one more time when he observed what he'd done to pat the head of the ugly statue with fondness I couldn't bring myself to fathom.

Everyone in this town had at least one screw loose.

Which had me thinking about the town, the state of affairs, how sad it would be, despite issues with the residents, this lovely little cottage might soon be a memory and a sprawling, modern resort in its place. "What will happen to this house if the hotel deal goes through?" I guessed correctly, already knew that since the Doiron's place was going to be razed to make way for the resort. Surely that meant this cottage, Annie and Henry's and probably many more along this shoreline would be gone in short order, garden gnomes, picket fences and all.

He started at the question, stuttering a little before pulling out his phone. Checked the screen, blanched slightly.

"Bad news?" I didn't mean to pry, was just trying to be polite. But when he looked up and met my eyes, his were angry and, might I say, a little afraid.

What message did he just receive that had him so worked up? I guess I'd never know, as he finally managed an answer, as unsatisfying as it turned out to be. "I have to run," he said. "Enjoy the rest of your evening." And hurried off through the gate, slamming it shut behind him.

Well, that was weird. I watched him go, bemused but relieved, to say the least, though I have to admit I stood there for a moment, half expecting some further interruption, ready with a reticent sigh and patience for the inevitable. Listened to the sound of his car retreating, no others approaching.

I was almost disappointed to be greeted with quiet, even from Annie, aside from the waves washing to the shore on the other side of the fence, the distant sound of someone mowing their lawn, faint squeals of happy kids playing in the water.

Huh. Maybe the Universe figured I'd finally earned a little peace and quiet. We'd just see how long it lasted.

Oh, for Heaven's sake, Persephone. Get a grip. Zephyr was turning me into a sad cynic, and I just wasn't going to let that become the norm.

Determined to make the most of it from now on, I tossed off any expectation of further disaster and chose to look on the freaking bright side before I curled up in the fetal position and cried on my pillow.

I took my time with dinner, tried a new, slower playlist with some old romantic favorites that had me singing along, slow dancing with myself over the hardwood floors. Not even the sharp pain in my baby toe could dampen my mood, though I did have to stop and pick out the sliver of glass I'd missed with the broom, a quick bit of doctoring including a cartoon pink bandage from my travel bag making me smile. It matched my nail polish.

My assembled dinner of charcuterie I put together myself ended up a lovely treat, a selection of cheeses and meats from the fridge Mitch dropped off, a few savory cracker offerings and a lovely red pepper jelly paired with a homemade mason jar of some kind of green hot sauce that tasted like cilantro and spring, satisfying my need for spiciness to counter the gin I sipped, rounding out my day rather nicely.

I even got to read, imagine that, and listen to some more music while finally taking advantage of the tub for a full hour while listening to a podcast I wanted to check out. Quickly ditching it, the alternate therapy method giving me eye rolls to the point I was telling the two hosts they were idiots (while they couldn't hear me, obviously, so who was the real idiot?) before shutting off the discussion early in favor of a quiet end to my soak.

By the time I settled back into the lawn

lounger—now returned safely to the garden thanks, I assumed, to Mitch and his meddling appearances—and looked up at the rising moon in the darkening sky, it was almost 9PM and I was close enough to sleepy I considered an early bedtime.

Imagine that. I might just make it through the evening without something horrible or exciting or frustrating happening.

Love you, Mom, Calliope texted. *Are you okay?*

She hadn't called. Chose to text. To give me space while still reaching out.

I did good with you, kid, I sent back.

So you seem to think, she responded a moment later. *Dad says he gets all the credit.*

Right, because he'd been around to raise her. Bite your tongue, Persephone. *You know what I think?* I sent a heart and a smiley face. *I think you came out exactly as amazing as you are, and your father and I only succeeded in staying out of your way long enough for you to turn into the truly wonderful and lovely young woman I adore to the bottom of my heart.*

She didn't reply for a long time. *Are you drinking?*

I laughed out loud at that. *I'll be home soon*, I sent. *Can't wait to hug you.*

You're sure you're okay? That was my only regret, Trent's worrywart buried deep in her heart.

I am, I sent. *Tell your father to mind his own business and I'll see you when I get home.*

Kk, she sent. *Night, Mom.*

I sent another heart emoji and sighed over the phone. That child needed to learn to relax a little or she'd have an ulcer at twenty-five. And it would be her father's fault.

Or her mother's for making her worry.

Enough of that. Time for bed and a deep, cleansing sleep and surely the sheriff would be amenable to my departure tomorrow. With that happy and hopeful thought in mind, I stood, stretched, rattling my empty gin glass before deciding against another.

My phone buzzed as I headed for the steps, catching me before I could climb them. I checked the message, toe scuffing against the side of the new gnome, tilting it and knocking it over in the process. Whoops. I ignored the ungainly statue in favor of the incoming, assuming it was Calliope again, or even Trent, only to find, to my surprise, an email from Ellen at town hall.

Apologies for the wait, she sent. *I took work home and thought of you just this minute. Happy property hunting and welcome to Zephyr!* Attached was a document labeled Zephyr Council Hotel Proposal.

Huh. I'd obviously misread Ellen's intentions and sent her a returned email with thanks before opening the file to have a look-see. Perused the contents with curiosity, the details of the proposal. Realized as I read the date Ellen sent me the wrong file. Almost messaged her until I read the last page.

The names written on the bottom of the document as the main contributors. Sheriff Perkins. Lou and Linda Savoy. And another that had me stop. Inhale a little sharply. Pause.

I had to be imagining things, jumping to conclusions again. Bent as I was pondering, slipping my phone into my pocket, and righted the statue at my feet. Noted, in my surprise, a footprint. Fresh. Familiar.

Not Kendall Doiron's.

And knew who killed him.

I heard a feline hiss and snarl, half-turned in surprise, but too late. Something struck the back of my head, stars flaring before darkness took me over, tumbling into black while my mind fought unconsciousness because I knew my attacker was the killer and if I let it take me, I was dead too.

And then, nothing.

And then, something. Sound, vibration, a bit of light. My equilibrium felt shot, wobbly, and it wasn't until I managed to blink a little, to open my eyes enough to see, I realized why. I lay on my side facing the door, kneeling on the floor in the front passenger's side of my own SUV, head and chest lying on the seat, holding me partially upright.

I almost groaned, held it in, the movement of the car, the rumble of the engine silencing me, bringing me back to consciousness despite the splitting headache and disorientation. Driving. We were driving.

Where?

The SUV turned rather sharply, something sliding out from under the seat and hitting my knee. Realized the flat, black rectangle was my phone. Almost wept in relief because I recognized at the same moment my hands were free. My attacker didn't expect me to wake up.

Do you have any idea how agonizing it could be to move slowly when time felt like it was running out and there was no way of knowing just how much was left before the end? I forced myself to move with utmost care, my left arm already partially dangling, letting it drop at last in the most natural way possible as we hit a fortuitous bump. Waited another horrifying and painful moment before I flipped my phone over on its side so the light wouldn't shine directly upward and keyed it on.

I couldn't see, but I knew who was at the top of my speed dial and, despite knowing it would terrify her—the exact reason she was the perfect choice—I called my daughter.

Just as the car skidded around another bend and Mitch spoke.

"I know you're awake," he said. Even as a distant and worried voice I hoped was quiet enough he didn't hear over the engine said, "Mom?"

CHAPTER SEVENTEEN

"Where are you taking me, Mitch?" I purposely raised my voice, hoping Calliope would hear me, knowing even if she couldn't make out what I was saying the worrywart her father built into her would mean she'd call him or at least the local authorities.

The question was, would she reach them in time to do any good?

"Mom, are you okay?" Why, in this of all times, was my daughter not acting on her usual state of nervousness when it came to me? Just a short time ago she was the consummate apprehensive mini version of Trent. What, had she suddenly grown out of her state of protectiveness? Just when I needed it most? "Are you playing a joke on me? This isn't funny." At least, I'm pretty sure that was what she said, the sound of her voice in and out as the phone slid around on the floor as we took another turn. I tried to look up, but my head ached so much my stomach rebelled, more stars rolling in, a groan finally escaping me.

"It'll be over soon." Mitch's voice held no expression, and even if I could have seen his face, I was sure he'd have had that dull and glassy stare of someone who'd been pushed so close to the edge emotion didn't register any longer. Honestly, it was too much effort to contemplate turning to observe when my only hope for rescue finally seemed to understand I was in trouble, Calliope's voice now panicked as I spoke myself.

"We're outside town," I said as loudly as I dared, risking another lift of my head to look out the window. Trees, just trees, though the road felt odd, bumpy and uncared for. "Are we in the woods?" Yes, I was being obvious, and no, I had no options and of course, I knew Mitch would catch on eventually.

What choice did I have?

"I didn't mean for it to come to this, you know." His voice dropped, the sound of a cough and then a throat clearing, his tone thick when he spoke again. What, tears at a time like this? Some murderer he was proving to be. "I only wanted to make our town a better place.

To improve our lives, to keep our young people from leaving."

"Like your wife and son left?" Their names had been on the document, right alongside his. Their life savings—including his son's college fund—dedicated to the hotel's development, that truth buried in the original file Ellen accidentally sent me.

A wife and son no longer living in Zephyr, according to Theresa Ellis, gone six months ago. And now I knew why.

The engine gunned a moment as if he reacted badly to my question. I held my breath and tried to sit up, knowing I risked passing out again but really needing to know where I was. The world went wonky for about ten seconds, the quiet pull of nothingness luring me back into blissful unknowing, but I won the battle against it, gulping air and pinching the inside of my forearm as hard as I could, the pain sharp enough to keep me functioning.

For now. No promises down the road, but it would do.

The light on my phone had gone out, the thing itself slid far enough under the seat I could no longer see it or hear my daughter. Had she hung up? Or was she on the landline at the house right now calling in the calvary? I had to believe the latter, blearily looking up, at last, to meet Mitch's eyes as I huddled in the narrow space between the seat and dash.

Tears tracked down his face, grim and grieving expression warped from this position, faint light from outside only increasing the weirdness of the shadowy and almost cartoonishly sinister cast the moon's illumination created. Because that silvery glow had nothing to do with streetlights. I was right, we'd left town limits. But how far out had we come? As we hit another bump, this one deep enough I cried out in agony and had to tip forward to rest my head before it exploded into a gazillion bits and shining pieces, I knew it had to be a road less traveled.

Which meant despite my attempt to save myself, it was very likely my daughter's call for help would end, not in my rescue, but the discovery of my body.

At least she'd have something to bury.

No. I was not giving up, not now. Pushed myself upright again, shimmied around just enough my knees hit the lever beneath to adjust the seat and shoved it back as far as it would go. Mitch's head whipped around, eyes black pits in the dark with only a faintly wet glimmer to them as the moonlight washed through the side window, the light moving around to the front of the car.

"We're heading east," I said then, with that same loudness, wincing and shaking my head to cover the volume with fake (okay, not so fake) disorientation. Wait, was that right? The moon rose in the east, didn't it? And it was early evening. I saw it rise last night over the water. Or was that tonight? Yes, tonight, though so hard to keep the details straight, to find clues to tell Calliope, but I had to keep trying.

I was not going to leave my daughter this way.

"I never thought you'd get caught up in this, I hope you know that." He was talking again but almost didn't seem to be speaking to me. Was he instead addressing his wife—what was her name, Sherry?—and their son? Isaac, right? "When I rented you the cottage, I thought I had time to make some quick cash before the deal went through. I needed that money, Persephone." He was talking to me after all.

"I know," I said. "For Isaac, right? You gave up his college fund for the hotel project."

Mitch twitched in the driver's seat, hands clenching the wheel, another bump making me whimper. But this time I held on, both palms pressed to the front of the seat, closing my eyes and praying for the pain to end. Which it mostly did, or at least became tolerable again, though my stomach rebelled firmly enough I was certain I wasn't going to last much longer.

A concussion, without a doubt. I needed medical attention immediately.

"I had to get you out of the cottage if you weren't going to pay," he said. "But Perkins wouldn't let you go, and I couldn't charge you." He wiped at his face with one hand. "I hoped you'd just leave, thought if I disturbed you often enough, you'd just leave."

"You threw the rock through the window," I said. It wasn't Kendall after all.

"Why didn't you just leave?" He almost wailed that at me, looking down as the moonlight finally reached full frontal and lit his desperate and panicked face. More tears, but not for me. "Perkins is nothing. He had zilch on you. You could have left, and everything would have been fine." He slammed one hand down on the wheel, anger flashing over his features. "But you didn't, you stayed. You stayed and you asked questions and you wouldn't leave it alone."

"You don't have to do this," I said. "You can just let me go now, Mitch. I'll leave, I promise." Right, like that was going to work.

He didn't seem to hear the request, lost in his own churning deep dive into the sort of plummeting despair that never ended well. "It's not fair," he groaned, lower lip trembling, waffling between grief and fury in flashing bits of terrifying meltdown that had me fighting for breath and any sense of calm. "They just had to say yes, that was all. No one expected them to say no. The whole town was invested, and they said *no*."

Mary and Kendall. My mind showed me the footprint in the garden, thought of Candace and her father. And made a connection I'd come to earlier and forgotten all about. Concussions will do that to you, I suppose.

"You pushed Mary off the ladder," I said.

He glanced at me, snarled. "She wouldn't listen to reason," he said. "I just wanted to talk to her, and she refused. All of my money, all of my son's money, was tied up in the deal. Not just mine, the whole town. And she wouldn't listen." I watched him snap all over again, saw the red rage cross over his face, sat there reliving the moment with him until he shuddered out of it and came back to me. At least, enough to focus on driving again, for which I was grateful. "I didn't mean to kill her. But she wouldn't talk to me."

"You heard Candace coming home and you ran," I said.

"To Sunshine," he said. "I heard her find Mary. Heard her calling for Kendall. There was always a part of me that feared he knew what I'd done. But he never turned me in so I just…" He left that hanging, wonder, bemusement replacing some of his rage.

"So why kill him now?" I shifted positions, reaching under the seat a little, fingers skimming for my phone. If I could find the GPS program, I could maybe have that sexy British boy tell Calliope where I was before Mitch could stop me.

He spun on me in a flash, so intense I froze, positive he'd read my mind or knew what I was up to somehow. Instead of stopping me, however, he spoke again, panic returned.

"I knew you would think that," he said. "I knew you'd jump to that conclusion. But I didn't kill Kendall, I swear. Yes, I pushed Mary and she fell, and the fall killed her." He clearly couldn't bring himself to say the words, that he was a murderer, and I didn't force him to. "But I had nothing to do with Kendall's death."

Wait a second. "You threw the rock," I said.

"I almost didn't," he said. "Someone was on the beach, I heard them arguing. Something about Mary. I thought it was about me, but they were too far away." He stopped talking a moment, a stricken look traveling over his features. "I couldn't tell the sheriff that." Perkins would wonder what Mitch was doing at the cottage at 2AM, the same time as the vandalism. "I couldn't back out then, though. I had to act. So, I threw the rock and ran," Mitch said. "That was it."

Voices on the beach. Arguing about Mary? So, who killed…?

Ah. I'd been right before, though the how was still a mystery. One I might not get to find the answer to unless I figured out a way to convince Mitch to let me go or my daughter saved my butt.

Despite my circumstance? The truth I now knew made me sad.

"Annie Layton saw you push Mary off the ladder," I said. "She thought you were Kendall."

Mitch glanced at me, shock now the dominant emotion. "Why didn't she say anything?"

She did. She just had the people and the timing wrong.

"You realize you let Candace think her father murdered her mother all this time?" I hadn't meant to get angry, but you know what? The man killed someone over money, scared the living daylights out of me, put me in an impossible position and then hit me on the back of the head and was now driving me who knew where to try to dispose of me. You bet I was angry. And while I was well aware the concussion wasn't helping matters, I wasn't in much of a state of mind to pull back or regulate my temper, so I didn't try. "You let an innocent young woman believe her father killed her mother. You're despicable."

Mitch's jaw set, jumped, his head shaking slowly back and forth. "It's not my fault," he said.

He'd never convince me otherwise.

"All for money, Mitch," I said.

"I'm bankrupt, don't you understand?" He shouted that into the cabin of the SUV, shaking so violently now I feared we'd run off the road. If we did, so be it. "My wife left, and my son went with her. I have nothing. Just that cottage and no tourists. You were going to save me, at least long enough for the deal to go through. I just needed a little good luck." He was crying again. "Just something to go my way, that's all." Mitch backhanded his wet cheeks, grim determination returning. "The deal is back on, though," he said then, turning the wheel, slowing the car as he went on. "The hotel chain agreed to honor our initial investments if we could get everyone to sign by this week." Now I knew who contacted them immediately after Kendall's death. "And everyone did."

"Candace," I said. "She sealed it."

He nodded, weak and wavering smile warring with what amounted to madness in his eyes as he parked the car, sat back, hands trembling in his lap. "You're all that stands between me and that luck, Persephone. I'm so sorry about this. You should have gone home when you had the chance." He swallowed hard, still staring, doing nothing, car running, his hesitation giving me an opening.

"It's a different thing," I said, soft and understanding, "reacting in anger, pushing a ladder in a fit of rage than it is to purposely end someone's life." I let that sink in a moment. "Isn't it, Mitch?"

"Ellen BCC'd us all you were inquiring." Was that the message he'd received, the one that had him angry and afraid? Had to be. "Then on the message she sent, the file." He sobbed then, his emotional instability my last indicator I wouldn't be getting through to him. He was just too far gone to reach. "The whole planning committee. When I realized she'd sent the wrong document, the old one, I knew you'd put it together." He finally pressed the button, the engine dying, the sudden quiet almost painful to my already throbbing head. "You're right, though. It is different. But I've come too far, and I've done too much, lost too much, to let that stop me." When he met my eyes for the last time, his were empty and flat. "I want you to know, you brought this on yourself."

And I thought I was the master of justifying crazy.

CHAPTER EIGHTEEN

At least we'd stopped, the constant bumps and jarring ride no longer contributing to the ache in my head. Not that I should have been happy, however, since the halt likely meant not only had the SUV come to the end of the line. But so had I.

I had to stop thinking that way, mind racing, muzzy from pain and still struggling through the fog of wobbles as Mitch opened the driver's door and got out, slamming it behind him. I took a peek out the window, clutching at the seat cushion, noted the darkness, no sign of a streetlight, trees and what looked like water. A railing.

A bridge.

And his plan of disposal suddenly came into sharp focus without him having to tell me what he was going to do.

I didn't expect him to open the back hatch, then return to the driver's side, pouring liquid all over the seat and floor. Until I noticed the label, realized it was the gin he'd bought, and the depth of his intention appeared. Not just get rid of me, but make it look like my own fault.

"There's a matching bottle you brought in the cottage," he said, tossing it to the passenger's seat, now empty. "Who's to say you didn't decide to go for a drive after having too much and ended up in the river?" He closed the driver's door again while I forced myself up in a single heave, twisting to sit in the seat, legs aching from the uncomfortable position I'd been in, now dealing with pins and needles along with the agony of my head pounding while circulation returned. Shaking hands grasped for the door, but he was already circling the front of the car, headlights shining on him, casting shadows upward to his grim face. I fumbled for the lock, flipped it open, but only in time for him to jerk the door wide.

"Time to go for a swim, Persephone," he said, leaning suddenly in, grabbing the bottle from the seat beside me, lifting it just enough I knew he planned to finish the job he'd started in the garden, a blow that would not only knock me out but be easily explained away after he forced the SUV with me in the driver's seat through the guardrail and into the river to drown.

There were moments in my life I recall time slowing down. Delivering Calliope, for example, that last push of agony and joy, when the entire Universe hung in on her first breath and cry of life. The time I went rock climbing with my friend, Lou Ellen, and fell, caught after a heartbeat of free fall by a guide rope and a handsome twentysomething kid who cheered me on when I refused to let it scare me. The long, silent and aching moment after I told Trent I wanted a divorce. Snippets of life, no more or less than a tick of the second hand, inconsequential in the grand scheme of linear forward motion. And yet, those instants clung to the edges of seconds, to the very coattails of time, lingering, hovering in an exhale of fear or hurt or ecstasy as reminders of how precious life really was.

Time suspended in that moment, Mitch's raised arm, the bottle, my frozen state of terror, the moonlight and the rushing river silent, everything sliding to a halt as panic grasped infinity's allotment and stilled.

Slammed to full speed again as a large, white ball of fur leaped from the back seat, hissing and snarling, and attacked Mitch with outstretched claws.

He fell back, out of shock more so than hurt. Didn't matter, the streak of fluff landing on the ground while I followed her, tumbling forward in a desperate move, falling on my hands and knees, hearing him grunt, backpedaling tripping him over a stone as he fell, too.

The only thing that mattered was escape, the hovering loss of time long gone, now sped to a frantic pace. Why then did my body feel encased in glue? My motions slow and scrabbling, my heaving breaths fighting rising hysteria, desperate to reach the side of the road, the trees, to get away as sobs tore my throat.

When he grabbed me, I screamed, the touch of his hand not so much painful as it was a culmination of horror. My life wasn't supposed to end like some Hollywood movie. I wasn't supposed to be dragged by my upper arm by a vice-like grip as I fought and yelled for help and stumbled my way to my feet only to fall again to the lip of the bridge. This couldn't be happening.

I looked up when he tossed me to the ground, releasing me to lean against the guard rail, the old bridge's wooden support giving way just a little. I hated the tears I couldn't control, fought the stampeding frenzy that tried to devour me, grappled with hysteria on the edge of my own madness as his fully consumed him, shining brightness of the headlights giving him a demonic half-face of a killer committed to my end.

He panted over me, catching his breath, glancing at the car. "I'll push it in after you," he said, but not to me, clearly working out his plan out loud, nodding to himself. "Smash the windshield. They'll think you weren't wearing a seatbelt and were thrown free of the car." Mitch returned his attention to me. "It'll be over fast. The river is rough and there are a lot of rocks." There was nothing left in his voice, no intonation, no threat or anger. Just an empty attempt at what? Reassurance? Comfort?

Wasn't working.

I had only one chance and I knew it. I would not go down like this. Fear or no fear, I would *not* die in the back of nowhere because I solved a murder.

Two murders. So there.

The moment Mitch drew a deeper breath, rest over, I stiffened, tensing, aching in my head worsening. I ignored it as best I could and watched as he bent to grab me.

Grabbed him instead. The shocked look on his face was almost worth it as I rolled sideways on my back, legs rising, feet catching him in the stomach. And, like a childhood game where one suspends the other by handholds and toes pressed to hipbones, I lifted him off the ground, grunting with the effort, before tilting my body sideways.

Toward the railing.

I never expected it to work. My last-ditch effort was simply an impulse, trust my gut moment. So, when he soared, hands reaching to catch something, anything, as he flew with near effortlessness into the dark, I gaped.

Sat up far quicker than was good for my head, crying out from the effort, but fast enough to watch as he fell, splashing abruptly into the river, the water carrying his thrashing body away.

Alive, still alive. I hadn't killed him as he'd planned to do to me. Why did I feel relief? Or maybe that emotion rose at the sound of distant sirens, of approaching headlights rushing through the trees toward me.

I turned slowly, resting against the wobbly rail, crying still but in relief, blessed relief. Opened my arms when she came trotting, cuddling close the purring cat who'd saved my life.

"Thanks, Bella," I whispered into her fur while the sheriff's car pulled up in a spray of gravel, the sound of voices calling my name ignored for the time being as I looked down into her green eyes. "I owe you one."

She head-butted her agreement before settling into my lap to wait for rescue.

CHAPTER NINETEEN

I knocked on the front door of the cute pink house, most of the pain muffled by drugs, enough I could function, at least. Sheriff Perkins insisted I spend the night in the small local hospital, something I didn't argue against, though I made sure one of his deputies took Belladonna home to Candace while the ambulance carried me away. Perkins also promised to take care of my car, though I cared less about the gin-soaked SUV and more about the fluff of white who'd done me a solid.

She was the hero of the story, that cat and my Calliope, so I couldn't just leave her out there in the dark woods, could I? She deserved a queenly police escort home if ever anyone did.

The remaining ache in my head wasn't

going anywhere, and neither was I, had convinced the sheriff without a lot of effort, surprisingly, to take me with him when I filled him in on the last piece of the puzzle. He'd driven, my car in the capable hands of the local detailing place, even arranged to have the town pay for it, imagine that. Was quiet but a far cry from the aggressively antagonistic and untrusting man I'd first met. Whether the truth about Mitch Arbor had shaken his faith or this trip to the pink gingerbread house on Daisy Lane changed his perspective, Sheriff Perkins seemed to have had a change of heart about me.

I'd take it.

The door opened after a moment, a hesitant and slow reveal, Henry on the other side, peering out at me in the morning sunlight, the sheriff standing behind me. I'd been surprised Perkins agreed to let me do the talking, though maybe it had something to do with the fact I'd not only helped him solve Mary Doiron's murder, I was about to reveal Kendall's too.

"Hello, Henry," I said. "Is Annie here?"

His wavering smile turned to instant worry. "She's resting," he said, tried to close the door. "Come back later."

But Perkins was already stepping up, his firm hand keeping it open, glancing at me and nodding.

"We have to talk to both of you, Henry," I said in my most empathetic voice, pulling out all the therapist stops on this one. "I think you know why we're here."

Tears welled in his pale eyes, spilled over wrinkled cheeks, unchecked as he sighed, nodded. Stepped back from the door, let us enter. Perkins removed his hat, face grim and sad while the sound of pattering footsteps had all three of us turn to look up the wooden staircase as Annie descended, grinning, almost girlish in her sundress and bare feet when she clapped her enthusiasm at our arrival.

"Visitors!" She stopped next to Henry, smacking him in the shoulder rather loudly. "Get them some tea, why don't you?" Her nasty attitude switched like a light fixture turning on, back to cheerful welcome. "Won't you come in?" She twirled in a pirouette, heading for the interior of the house while Henry watched her go, the sound of her humming a tragic counterpoint to the reason we were there.

"She's sick, you see," he said in the weariest voice I'd ever heard. His pleading expression was for both of us, as he looked back and forth between me and the sheriff. "Her mind is going. She doesn't know what she's doing or saying anymore." He sighed, shoulders rounded forward under his faded plaid shirt, tears wetting the collar of the white t-shirt he wore underneath. "Not anymore."

"I'm sorry, Henry," Perkins said, "but we have no choice here."

Henry turned, shuffled off after his wife, while my heart broke for the both of them.

We found her sitting in the sunshine, in their little garden, surrounded by flowers. I took note of the bench by the fence, the very thing she'd used to spy on me. Dirty footprints from her bare feet marked the surface, little lines of sand left behind from her strolls on the beach.

She beamed up at us, though when Henry sat next to her at the little table, she smacked him again. "Where's my breakfast?"

He didn't say anything, just sat there, crying and despondent, while she tsked at him before fluttering her eyelashes at us.

"Annie." Sheriff Perkins cleared his throat, glanced at me again. So, he was uncomfortable confronting them, was he? Well, they were neighbors, people he'd known his whole life and I highly doubted he'd ever expected to be in this situation.

I took over immediately, sitting next to Annie on the other side, taking her hand, smiling in return. "Hello, Annie," I said. "Do you remember me?"

"Of course, I do, Mary." She snorted, wry grin host to just a hint of bitterness. "I told you to mind that husband of yours, didn't I?" Annie leaned back, crossing her arms over her narrow chest, her foot bobbing over her knee, pale skin showing faint blue veins beneath her wrinkles. She'd failed to brush her hair that morning, the halo-like wispiness letting sunlight through, surrounding her in a crown of golden light. "I hate how he yells all the time. All the time." She flicked her fingers at me before crossing her arms again.

"Annie, dearest," Henry said then. "They want to know what happened the other night. To Kendall."

Annie's pale eyes widened just a little, hands falling free, clasping in her lap as though she cupped an object. I knew where her mind just went, knew exactly what it was she imagined she held because she'd used it to kill Kendall Doiron.

The little gnome she claimed was hers.

"You came into the garden that night," I said, soft and light, no accusation, just an attempt to guide her memory, shattered by her illness but still there if I was careful.

Annie nodded slowly, staring into the

distance. "I wanted Lewis back," she said, voice almost normal. "He died so young you know. Just an infant." And now I had that answer, too. "But I saw him in the garden. Why was he in the garden?" Her hands clutched closed, and she looked down into her lap, startled to find nothing there. "I want him back." Annie's sharp gaze rose to mine again. "He was going to take Lewis from me, I knew it, Mary. He killed you, you know." She blinked, flinched as she looked away, frowning, memory torture for her. "He killed you and he was going to kill me, wasn't he? Steal Lewis and leave me to die?" That new petulant expression only increased my compassion as she licked her lips, bemused, confused. "He killed Mary," she said, suddenly utterly lucid, "and when I saw him on the beach, I told him so. He was angry." She shuddered. "He called me a liar, shoved me." She rubbed at her upper arm, hidden by her sweater and likely disguising a bruise. "I dropped the gnome." Not her deceased son any longer. She burst into tears then, folding in half, sobbing as she clutched at her midsection as though in agony. "He bent," she managed through her weeping, "he tried to pick it up. I pushed him back." Annie's hysteria faded as she sat upright again, met my eyes with hers devoid of anything now, the moment of her lucidity leaving her. "He fell, hit his head on the gnome." She turned abruptly to Henry, smacked him. "Where's my breakfast?"

I exhaled slowly, did my best to hold back my own tears, the tragedy of the death of Kendall Doiron finally fully revealed.

"It was an accident," Henry said then, his pathetic panic returned. "Surely you see that?"

"Who dragged the body into the water, Henry?" That was Perkins, unrelenting though visibly disturbed by what he'd heard.

The old man stilled, looked at his wife who now hummed softly to herself, smiling and picking at a thread on her sweater. "I did," he said. "I found her just as Kendall fell, saw the whole thing. He was already dead when I reached her." Henry's hands wrung in his lap a moment before he grasped the arms of his chair for support, arthritic knuckles white as he squeezed. "Please, I only wanted to protect my wife."

"We will, of course, take her condition into account," Perkins said. "But it's obvious she needs more care than you can give her, Henry. And there's the fact you tried to cover up the accident. It can't stand, I'm sorry."

Henry nodded, reaching for Annie's hand. She jerked hers out of his grip and frowned at him, sticking out her tongue. "I know," he said.

"I've known for a while. It's for the best. But I love her. She's my everything." He broke down then, weeping into his hands, while Annie smacked him.

"Where's my breakfast?"

CHAPTER TWENTY

I closed the rear hatch on my luggage, the cat carrier Candace gave me belted into the back seat, though I highly doubted my guest would willingly use it. Belladonna had already settled on the passenger's side, tucked into the safety booster seat I'd installed for her. My plan to take a slow drive home had morphed yet again into a direct return so my hitchhiker could get settled into her new digs at my house. Um, soon to be her house, the freeloader.

She was the first pet I'd had in my life since I met Trent, his allergies always keeping us from furry friends at home. Having a cat was going to make things interesting and I almost giggled with evil anticipation he'd avoid my place like the plague with Bella around.

Silver linings, people. Silver linings.

Sheriff Perkins pulled up as I dropped the keys to the cottage in the mailbox, not sure what else to do with them now that Mitch wasn't here. The sheriff tipped his hat as he came up the drive, his attitude utterly different now, even pleasant. The evolution of our antagonism only improved after the ambulance arrived to take Annie away yesterday, Henry going with her, still weeping while she clapped and treated it like a game. I suppose to her it was. At least one of them was happy leaving their cute little house.

It was likely the last time either of them would ever live in it.

The sheriff peeked in at the sleeping cat waiting for me to hit the road, tapping the glass to get her attention, a fact she ignored with the single-minded intensity of a feline enjoying her new throne in air-conditioned comfort.

"Bella, huh?" He nodded kindly, smiled. "Candace's been talking about finding her a good home for a while. Nice to see she found one." He squinted up at Sunshine Cottage, taking a moment before going on. "Sorry to hear you're leaving so soon, though I get it." Wow, things really *had* changed. The part of me that wanted people to like me had a nice sigh of relief while the snarky side—the dominant side—relented and forgave and understood.

"And for the reception when you arrived." Nice of him to recognize it and apologize for it. He shrugged a little, grinned. "We're friendly folk, honest. It's just been a rough year around here and it's been tough to see any way out of it. Until now."

I accepted the apology gracefully, smiling back. "Things are about to change for the better, from what I understand."

His grin spread, shoulders going back, the kind of defeated air about him I only now recognized dominated his entire being since we'd met gone and done away with. I guess knowing the money you lost was about to be recovered and that hope sat on the horizon in the guise of a resort had that kind of influence. "The hotel is moving forward," he said, repeating what I already heard from a quick trip to the market this morning, Theresa Ellis stepping out from behind her booth to hug me and wish me well. Two cartons of fresh strawberries and a box of veggies waited on the floor in the back seat for my arrival home and I had a feast planned for all of it. She'd shared the good news, the air of the whole town changed, shifted to optimism and a zinging delight that triggered my happily ever after endorphins. "They're even honoring all of our investment money. I'm just grateful they're still willing to work with us. And once the place is up and running, our shares will make it all worthwhile."

"That's really great news, sheriff," I said. "Congratulations. Maybe I'll come back for a visit once the hotel is done." I only made that mention to be nice. Because I'd already decided I would never again set foot in Zephyr for any reason whatsoever.

"I think you'll find things a lot different around here," he said, his good humor actually making a small dent in my determination to put this place in my rearview. "Oh, thought you'd want to know, the park ranger boys found Mitch this morning, early. He was a bit beat up from the ride downriver, but he'll survive. To stand trial for murder." Maybe Perkins wasn't a bad sheriff, after all. "You know, you raised a heck of a kid, in case you missed it. If she hadn't called me three times in a row and demanded I track your GPS, we'd have found you after the fact, not Mitch."

My plan had worked, though Calliope and her tech-savvy saved the day. I didn't realize she could have the SUV located thanks to her access to my app. Might have been annoyed at that previously, but not under this particular circumstance. "I'm grateful for her every day," I said with utmost sincerity. Refused her insistence she drive up only to come home with me. Could still hear her frustration when I thanked her, told her I loved her and hung up on her.

Yes, she'd saved my life. And I'd hug the heck out of her when I got home. But I would be going home on my own. With the other shero in my life, that was.

The sound of a door closing, and a call of hello had us both turning to find Candace coming up the driveway on her side, circling to join us. She nodded to the sheriff who tipped his hat back, their mutual happiness lifting my spirits despite my lingering headache. The doctor had cleared me but warned me I'd be a bit out of sorts for a few weeks, the reminder of the attack popping up every time I moved my head too fast.

At least he said I could drive. If I'd had to have my daughter or ex-husband come all this way just to take me home, I'd have chosen to stay as long as I needed for recovery.

Stubborn? You better believe it. I didn't start this new life of mine just to fall back into the way things used to be. I was even more determined now to show Trent and Calliope life had changed. For the better. For all of us.

"Congratulations on the new job," Perkins said to Candace who laughed a nervous little giggle though she seemed excited more than scared.

"The hotel offered me a management position," she said. "I'm going to be moving to Bangor for training for the next month or so, and when I'm done, I'll be placed at a variety of their hotels and resorts so when the one here is complete, I can be part of the team."

"That's fantastic," I said, accepting her impulsive hug with one of my own. "Good for you, Candace."

"When I get back to Zephyr," she whispered in my ear, "everything will be changed. Including me. And I can start fresh."

Didn't I just know how she felt? Going home to Wallace hadn't been something I'd looked forward to when I'd hit the road just a few short days ago. But my experience had shifted everything, and I couldn't wait to see what new adventures lay ahead.

Perkins left with a hearty wave and a final hat tip, Candace lingering while the purring engine and hum of air conditioning ensured Belladonna's comfort for the duration of the conversation. I found I was surprised I'd miss the lovely young woman who looked so renewed, almost like a totally different person.

"Thank you, Persephone," she said, tears rising to her eyes, though her smile remained if a little trembly. "If you hadn't…" she cleared her throat, looked away a moment, then reached out and took my hand. "I'd have spent the rest of my life thinking my father killed my mother. Thank you for taking that burden from me."

I hugged her again, promised to stay in touch (which we wouldn't more than likely, but it was a nice sentiment) and finally climbed into the driver's seat, the faint scent of cleaner lingering. The detailer had done a great job removing the gin, not to mention doing it quickly. I waved to Candace as I backed out onto the lane and headed for the edge of town, reaching over to stroke Belladonna's soft ear.

She purr/meowed a question when I disturbed her, green eyes in slits.

"Sorry," I said. "Have a nice nap. I'll just be over here driving."

She yawned hugely, sharp teeth bright white against her pink tongue.

"Hope I'm not boring you," I said. "And I'm already turning into a crazy cat lady who talks to her pet like you understand. Awesome. Does that mean you're my starter kit and I'll be an old broad with a hoarder issue someday?"

Bella just blinked at me, before settling back into sleep.

"I don't mind boring," I said. "I think I've

had my fill of bodies and close calls, too, if that's okay with you?"

The cat sneezed, a soft and delicate sound before she murmured something that sounded far too much like, "No promises."

Great. And here I'd just had my head examined.

Grinning, I pulled onto the freeway and aimed for home.

Looking for more from Persephone Pringle? You're in luck! Book two, **Urn Your Keep**, is available right now!

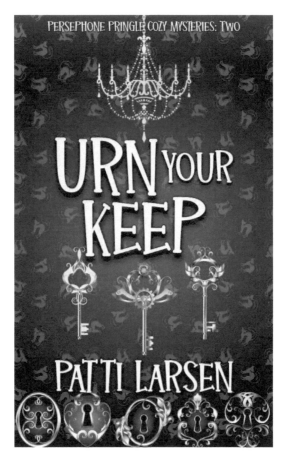

ABOUT THE AUTHOR

Everything you need to know about me is in this one statement: I've wanted to be a writer since I was a little girl, and now I'm doing it. How cool is that, being able to follow your dream and make it reality? I've tried everything from university to college, graduating the second with a journalism diploma (I sucked at telling real stories), am an enthusiastic member of an all-girl improv troupe (if you've never tried it, I highly recommend making things up as you go along as often as possible) and I get to teach and perform with an amazing group of women I adore. I've even been in a Celtic girl band (some of our stuff is on YouTube!) and was an independent filmmaker. You can check out the whole Lovely Witches Club series for free at:

https://lovelywitchesclub.com.

My life has been one creative thing after another—all leading me here, to writing books for a living.

Now with multiple series in happy publication, I live on beautiful and magical Prince Edward Island (I know you've heard of Anne of Green Gables) with my multitude of pets.

I love-love-love hearing from you! You can reach me (and I promise I'll message back) at https://patti@pattilarsen.com/home. And if you're eager for your next dose of Patti Larsen books (usually about one release a month) come join my mailing list! All the best up and coming, giveaways, contests and, of course, my observations on the world (aren't you just dying to know what I think about everything?) all in one place:

https://bit.ly/PattiLarsenEmail.

Last—but not least!—I hope you enjoyed what you read! Your happiness is my happiness. And I'd love to hear just what you thought. A review where you found this book would mean the world to me—reviews feed writers more than you will ever know. So, loved it (or not so much), your honest review would make my day. Thank you!

Made in United States
Troutdale, OR
06/18/2023

10669754R00106